HOLD ME CLOSE

A LODGE SERIES NOVEL

J.H. CROIX

This is a work of fiction. Names, characters, businesses, places, events and incidents are either the products of the author's imagination or used in a fictitious manner. Any resemblance to actual persons, living or dead, or actual events is purely coincidental.

Copyright © 2017 J.H. Croix

Cover design by Najla Qamber Designs

❁ Created with Vellum

To leaps of faith.

Sign up for my newsletter for information on new releases &
get a FREE copy of one of my books!

http://jhcroixauthor.com/subscribe/

Follow me!
jhcroix@jhcroix.com
https://amazon.com/author/jhcroix
https://www.bookbub.com/authors/j-h-croix
https://www.facebook.com/jhcroix

CHAPTER 1

*I*vy Nash waited in the sleek waiting room at Off the Grid Engineering and nervously fiddled with her cluster of silver bracelets. She'd gotten the email inviting her for an interview a full two weeks after her application. Whoever wrote it didn't get points for warm and friendly because it had been short and to the point, simply asking if she could attend an interview at a single time. It was now another week later, and she was waiting anxiously to get this over with. She tried to recall the last time she'd actually attended an interview and thought it must've been when she waited tables at a local pizza place in college. After that, she'd done one work-study program after another to pay for her education before accepting a faculty position in the same university where she completed her doctorate. She was entirely out of her element here. She wasn't one to try to sell herself. She preferred to show what she could do, but she didn't think that was how interviews worked.

Off the Grid was nearly the opposite of the stuffy academic environment she'd left behind. Its owner, Owen

Manning, was renowned in the engineering field. He'd been a shooting star in academia before he abruptly resigned his position on the faculty at United Technology and started his own company. He was dedicated to engineering eco-friendly, sustainable energy production and was constantly in the news pushing his latest innovation. He didn't seem to do anything by the book and had recently relocated his entire firm to Alaska over a year ago. It was pure luck for Ivy that Off the Grid happened to be in Diamond Creek, Alaska where her brother lived.

Rumor had it, Owen loved to ski. Diamond Creek was home to Last Frontier Lodge, a renowned world-class ski lodge where her brother Cam Nash worked. At the moment, it was hard to believe she was in Diamond Creek, a charming tourist town. Off the Grid was situated on the far side of town as high into the mountains as Last Frontier Lodge was. It was a state of the art facility with a sleek, modern feel and massive walls of windows. The spectacular beauty of the area was on vivid display with views of the mountains, Kachemak Bay and glaciers every which way she turned. The waiting room was painted in cool shades of violet and blue with black leather chairs for seating.

Ivy took another shaky breath, trying to quell the tension inside. She knew she was qualified for this job. She'd never doubted her intelligence and ability to work hard, but it wasn't her nature to boast. She needed this job and she really, really wanted it. All she wanted was a job where she could dig into the projects she loved and help design better technology for the world. There weren't many of those around, so she was crossing her fingers she could pull this interview off.

On the heels of another deep breath, a door to one side of the waiting room opened and Owen Manning stepped through. Her belly somersaulted and heat suffused her. She'd seen him in enough media interviews to know exactly who he was. She'd known he was handsome, but she'd been entirely unprepared to meet him in person. He had jet-black hair that curled at the edge of his collar and dark blue eyes. His features were strong and chiseled, and he was tall, his presence taking over the room the moment he stepped into it.

"Ivy Nash?" Owen asked.

She nodded quickly. A long moment passed while she tried to beat back her body's powerful reaction to Owen.

Owen arched a brow, at which point she realized she was still seated. She jumped up quickly. "I'm Ivy." She took a few steps across the room and held her hand out.

Owen reached out and clasped her hand, giving it a quick, firm shake. "Owen Manning," he said, his tone brusque.

His touch was like a shock to her system. His hand engulfed hers, warm and strong, and heat surged through her. She took a breath and forced herself to look up at him. Out of all of her worries about navigating this interview, she hadn't considered what to do if her body went haywire like this. His eyes flicked to hers, something she couldn't identify flashing in the depths of his gaze. He slowly released her hand and turned smoothly to hold the door open.

He gestured for her to pass through, so she did, her pulse beating wildly with each step. Once she stepped past him, she paused in the hallway while he closed the door. The hall was all glass on the side facing the mountains. She forced herself to focus on a mountain peak in the distance, trying to slow her pulse and calm her rapid, shallow breathing.

Owen stepped past her. "Follow me," he said, his words clipped.

She immediately began following him. His stride was long, so while he appeared to stroll down the hall, she felt like she was almost running. His shoulders stretched against the fabric of the navy jersey shirt he wore. She hadn't expected a business here to include people dressed in suits, but she also hadn't expected it to be quite so casual. Owen looked as if he'd stepped out of the pages of an outdoor magazine. Aside from his casual shirt, he wore a pair of faded jeans that outlined his muscled legs and a pair of well-worn leather boots.

The hall had a few doors along the way, all closed. When they reached the end of the hall, he opened the single door there and gestured for her to step through. She'd managed to get her pulse somewhat under control on the walk here, but the moment she had to pass by him, feeling the heat emanating from his body, it went wild again. She stepped into what must be his office. It was situated on the corner of the building with two walls of windows floor to ceiling offering a near-panoramic view of the area with the mountains to one side and Kachemak Bay glittering under the sun to another. There was no desk in here, but a large table with drafting paper, two laptops and a computer tablet scattered across its surface. The table was in the corner opposite the windows. In the windowed corner was a small round table with several comfortable chairs encircling it. Owen gestured to that area. "Have a seat."

Ivy thanked the universe she had manners because she moved on autopilot to the chairs and sat down, clutching the folder that held her resume and several summaries of projects she'd worked on so far. Owen sat down across from her and leaned forward, resting his elbows on his knees. His expression was like a stone wall, giving nothing away.

"You need to know I tend to make decisions quickly. I asked you to come to this interview because I've already made my decision. Your graduate and doctoral work was almost exclusively focused on what we do here. Your academic references are outstanding, and rumor has it you're easy to work with. Considering that engineers can be prone to arrogance and aren't the most social creatures, you score high for that. My only question for you is this: why are you leaving the academic world?"

Ivy stared at Owen, taken aback by his brusque tone and so startled by his words that she was silent for a long moment. He'd done a remarkable job of getting her mind off of thinking all kinds of thoughts about his body by asking the one question she hoped no one would ask in this new job search of hers. Though she'd mentally prepared herself for this question, she couldn't lie, but she also didn't want to discuss what actually happened in her last position. She hewed as close to the truth as possible. "All I want is to work in research and development. I'd hoped academia would offer me what I wanted, but I found the environment not what I was hoping for. I have, of course, heard about Off the Grid and the work you're doing. When I saw this position, I decided to try to make the leap. The fact that I have family here also made it an easy choice."

Once her words, which she had practiced in her head many times, came out, she breathed a sigh of relief. Everything she'd said was true. She simply hadn't elaborated on the details about the 'environment' she'd been forced to deal with. She hoped what she said would satisfy Owen. She wished she could read him better, but when she looked back into his eyes, all she saw was blue. Not a flicker of a reaction to her, or anything she'd said. He'd just told her he planned to hire her. She should be excited, but instead she wanted to flee the building, run from this wild attraction she couldn't seem to corral while he sat across from her—so calm, cool and collected, she was surprised she didn't feel a chill in the air.

* * *

OWEN WATCHED Ivy Nash while she spoke, doing his damnedest to keep his eyes on her face and away from her breasts. She wore some kind of silky cream-colored blouse. It wasn't tight, but the slip and slide of the silk as she gestured with her hands offered glimpses of the shadowed valley between her generous breasts. He couldn't say he'd had any expectations about what Ivy would look like, but he definitely hadn't expected to take one look at her and have his brain fuzz out. Pure habit got him through the motions of introductions and down the hall to his office. It was true he tended to be blunt and to the point, but he was in rare form right now because he could barely focus.

Ivy's name had blipped on his radar before she'd ever applied for the position here. As he'd just told her, her work as she made her way up the ladder of graduate school and onto her doctorate had mostly been on engineering self-sustaining energy. She'd done some engineering work for NASA on ways to lengthen battery life for various instruments used in rockets. He'd read a few of her papers and been intrigued. She was clearly bright, focused and cared about her work. Yet, he'd had no clue how she looked. Her amber hair fell in loose waves around her shoulders. Her eyes, like warm cognac, were wide and tilted up at the corners. And her mouth, holy hell her mouth. Her lips were full and perfectly bow shaped. She had a dimple on one side of her mouth, which made him want to lean over and kiss it. Her rectangular black glasses served to add a dash of illicit naughtiness—only because they made her look like his sexiest librarian fantasy come to life.

He had to force his attention to the moment. She'd just answered his only question. He distantly heard her explanation over the static in his brain, but he didn't have it in him to ask her again. He knew from her academic work that he wanted to hire her, so he would. This 'interview' was nothing more than a formality. His brain grasped onto the fact that she mentioned she had family here.

"You say you have family here?" he asked, figuring he needed to say something to look halfway polite.

Ivy looked relieved with his question, which piqued his curiosity. "My brother moved up here about a year ago. He runs the ski instruction program over at Last Frontier Lodge."

Owen's brain clicked into gear. "Ah, Cam Nash is your brother?"

Ivy nodded, a wide smile gracing her face and bringing out her tempting dimple. He kept his attention on her face, which should have been less distracting than her breasts, but he was finding it didn't really matter where he looked when it came to her—need galloped through him heedless of his mental attempts to corral it. *Focus, focus, focus.* He chanted silently and tried to keep the conversation on track. "One of the reasons I moved Off the Grid here was because I wanted to be able to engineer technology that could withstand harsh weather. The other was because I love to ski. Your brother's reputation precedes him. You ski?"

"Oh yeah. Not quite like Cam. I'm definitely slower, but I love it. Diamond Creek's a pretty amazing place for your company. How'd you find it?"

"I visited Alaska a few times when I was in college and fell in love with it. When I first started Off the Grid, I went with what was convenient. At the time, that was Boston because I was at United Tech. When we started doing well enough to need more space, I decided I wanted to be where I wanted to be. I flew out here to ski two years ago and figured it'd be hard to find a better place. Simple as that."

She nodded and fiddled with several silver bracelets on her wrist. "Well, Diamond Creek is certainly beautiful, and you just might have the best view around up here."

He chuckled. "We do have a great view, but it's easily as good in other areas around town."

When she nodded politely again, it occurred to him he hadn't officially told her he planned to hire her. For a flash, he wondered if maybe he should reconsider. He hadn't figured this wild, pounding attraction to her into the equation. His body was nearly humming from the electric shock of lust she elicited. With his body having a mind of its own, he was thrown off kilter and he didn't like it. He wasn't one to be swayed by the messy vagaries of lust—too complicated and confusing. He mentally shook himself. It would pass. It would have to. He needed another researcher, and she met every mark he'd set and then some.

"So, back to you. As far as I'm concerned, the job's yours. You can start whenever you're ready. Do you have any questions about the pay and benefits?"

Those stunning cognac eyes of hers widened slightly and her breath drew in sharply. His body tightened, and he forced himself to take a slow breath.

"Oh. That's it?"

"That's it. I'm familiar with your work, so I know you'll be a great asset. If you need some time to think about it..."

She shook her head, the tousled waves of her hair swinging softly. "No, no. I'd love to work here. I don't mean to sound silly, but I've only had one position since I finished my doctorate. Should I talk to someone in human resources if I have questions about the benefits or anything like that?"

He felt a disconcerting sense of warmth and protectiveness toward her. She was so open, so not calculating, so not so many things he had quickly tired of in academia – the constant ego battles and jousting for leverage. He looked over at her, catching her eyes and instantly locking into them. Electricity arced between them, so hot and fast, he could almost feel the heat in the air around them.

"HR here is Joan. She came with the company from

Boston and has since decided she lived in Alaska in another life and finally found her home."

He stood. "Come on. I'll take you down to meet her." He needed to do something other than stare at Ivy, so introducing her to Joan would give him something to do.

Not much later, he stood by the entrance and watched Ivy walk to her car, her hips swaying with each step. He wondered if he'd just lost his mind.

CHAPTER 2

The door closed shut behind her with a soft click. Ivy took a few steps into the room she'd just been told was her office. Joan from HR had spent the morning with her, reviewing all the forms she needed to sign, taking her around Off the Grid, and introducing to her to anyone they passed by. Ivy had yet to see Owen face to face again and was both relieved and disappointed. In the week since her interview, she'd been batting him out of her thoughts time and again. Every time she recalled how it felt to be in the same room as him, her skin flushed from head to toe, the simple recollection of his effect on her a visceral experience. When Joan walked her down the hall where she knew Owen's office to be, anticipation had rushed through her. His door was closed, but she could see him through the glass. He stood in front of the table with multiple computer screens on in front of him, his back to the door. His muscles flexed under his shirt as he reached across the table. Ivy had torn her eyes away. She was losing it over her new boss's back when she wasn't even in the same room.

Just when she wondered where Joan might be taking

her, seeing as Owen's office was at the end of the hallway, Joan opened the door closest to his and gestured inside. "Your office! I have to run to catch a conference call, so I'll leave you here to get settled. I'll come find you in a bit for lunch." At that, Joan hurried away. The door seemed to have a mind of its own and closed quietly without any impetus.

Ivy spun in a slow circle. The room felt like a blank slate, however somehow there was a warmth to it. It had floor to ceiling windows on one side, offering a view of the mountains with a glimpse of the bay through two peaks in the distance. They didn't seem to use desks here. Her office had a smaller version of the large worktable in Owen's office. There were two chairs situated by the windows with a low table between them. Although the entire building was modern and sleek, the space screamed comfort with its furnishings. The chairs in her office were plush and comfy, so spacious she could easily imagine curling up with her research for hours on end. A counter ran the length of the wall adjacent to Owen's office. It appeared she had her own personal coffee maker and teapot, complete with a single burner oven, microwave and tiny refrigerator masked by its cabinet style door.

Ivy hadn't thought much about what to bring other than her papers and books. Joan had already made arrangements to have her few boxes carted into her room. With her thoughts buzzing with the anticipation of starting a new job, living in a new place and her entirely inappropriate attraction to Owen, she was uncertain just what to do. She'd been driven intellectually for so many years, it had never occurred to her there would be a pause. Her pause had only lasted a month, yet she felt completely lost. Academia had been her home, or so she'd hoped it would be. A wave of bitterness rose inside. She'd chosen to leave her last job and she didn't doubt her decision for a minute, but it still bit at her that she'd felt forced to walk away from the research she loved.

She shook her head sharply. She needed something to latch onto, not to dwell on the past. It's just that she'd plastered all kinds of hopes and dreams onto that job and had to leave them behind along with everything else. With another spin to look around, she strode briskly to the boxes. A short while later, she'd added a few personal touches to her office and placed her books on the book shelf tucked into the corner behind her work table. She hadn't brought her own laptop, although she belatedly realized she probably should've. It would give her something to focus on while she waited. She was anxious to dive into the actual work here.

Restless, she paced slowly back and forth in front of the windows, almost jumping when there was a soft knock on the door. "Come in," she called out, assuming it was Joan.

The door opened on a whisper, and Owen stood there. Once again, she was reminded of the power of his physical presence. His tall, muscled frame filled the doorway. Those dark blue eyes of his landed on her. Her pulse bolted to a gallop, and her brain fuzzed. For a moment, he was quiet and simply looked at her. She hadn't paid much attention to her appearance because she'd been so anxious about coming here today. She was suddenly self-conscious. She wore a pair of black silky pants that swung around her ankles and a cashmere sweater that fit loosely. Owen held her gaze, the distance between them sparking to life. He dipped his head in a subtle nod.

"I hear Joan took you on a tour this morning. Do you have everything you need?" he asked as he stepped into her office.

He wore a long-sleeved cotton t-shirt, which his muscled chest filled out nicely, and faded jeans with worn leather boots. Her skin prickled everywhere, and she could hardly catch her breath. She belatedly realized he'd asked her a question. "Joan was great. She took me all over and made sure I met anyone we saw. I'm not sure if I missed anyone, but I'm sure I'll meet everyone eventually. I don't think I need anything. I suppose I'm wondering when I can get to work."

She fiddled with her silver bracelets, a nervous habit she'd never been able to break. Owen took another few steps into the room until he reached her side. "I hope you enjoy the view," he said with a nod toward the windows. As before, he felt remote and cool. He was polite enough, but with her body nearly on fire, his response to her only heightened how wildly out of control she felt.

"Of course. Is it my imagination or does every room in this building have a view?"

The slightest smile curved his lips, finally a chink in his armor. "Not your imagination. I figured we should make the best of the location. Even the bathrooms have a view."

Ivy felt herself start to smile and tried to stop it, but she couldn't. "I noticed."

She stood there smiling back at him until she realized what she was doing. The slightest smile from him made her goofy. She tore her eyes free and stared out over the view. Snow capped the peaks of the mountains. It was late winter with spring somewhere ahead, or so her brother promised her. Having grown up in Utah, she was accustomed to mountains and snow, although Cam had prepared her to expect winter in Alaska to last a tad longer than in Utah. Restless, she looked back to Owen. "So when will I be able to start working?"

He arched one of his dark brows. "Well, everyone who's ever worked with you told me you're an incredibly hard worker. I suppose I figured most people enjoyed a slow start to work. Joan wanted the morning to take care of HR stuff. She was supposed to be in charge of lunch, but the school called her to pick up her daughter. Something about a fever. I figured I'd take you to lunch instead. I can give you a rundown on our latest projects. Ready?"

Ivy was flustered beyond flustered and all Owen was doing was standing beside her. Lunch, right. He wanted to take her to lunch. She supposed her new boss taking her to lunch was perfectly normal, but her body was tingling and she'd have to find a way to breathe more effectively around him if she ever expected to get anything done. On the heels of a shallow breath, she nodded. "Sure."

She looked around for her purse and coat and followed him down the long hallway, carefully keeping her eyes on the spectacular view rather than him.

* * *

OWEN LOOKED across the table at Ivy. She was looking out the window, her eyes following the flight of an eagle that had just lifted off from the rocky beach and flew low across the water. Joan had insisted he take Ivy somewhere for lunch when she had to leave to pick up her daughter and further ordered him to be nice. "She's nervous. I can tell, so don't do your whole distant thing," Joan had said.

"Distant thing?" he'd asked in return.

"The thing where you're so focused on work, you barely bother to look at anyone. You've a heart of gold, but hardly anyone knows it. I like Ivy, and I don't want you to scare her off," Joan had said sternly before racing out the door to pick her feverish daughter up from school.

Joan had been with Off the Grid since the beginning, back when it was nothing more than a one-room office in the third story of an old building in Boston. Joan had been the first person Owen hired when he realized he needed help handling the logistics of the business. She was loyal, an incredibly hard worker and one of the best people he knew.

She was also one of the few people in his life now who'd known him before his parents died. Sixteen years ago, he'd been in his freshman year of college when he'd received a call early one morning. His parents had died of carbon monoxide poisoning during the night—an all too common occurrence, and one that ripped the foundation out from under his life. Joan was a family friend and had been his mother's receptionist in her accounting business.

While his mother had been a mentor to Joan, Joan in turn became one to him. She and her husband had insisted he stay with them during holidays after that, becoming the family he'd lost in many ways. Joan knew quite well that Owen could be distant. He'd come from a warm, loving family. As such, if there was one thing he didn't ever want to experience again, it was the pain of a loss like that. So, he was distant. It worked for him. Throwing himself into academics had saved his sanity after the painful loss of his parents. Their death also became the impetus that drove his engineering work. He was determined to provide cost-effective alternatives to energy that didn't hold the potential for death.

He gave himself a mental shake. He knew why Joan was being bossy with him about Ivy. She'd liked Ivy the first time she met her last week and was bound and determined to make sure he kept good employees. Engineers were hard to come by, particularly ones who specialized in the field of alternative energy and who were actually pleasant to work around. Ivy was unusual in that respect, or so her references indicated.

With Ivy absorbed in the view, he took a moment to look at her. Her amber hair was spun into a knot atop her head today with tendrils escaping and framing her face, one curl twining around a temple on her glasses. He'd convinced himself in the week since he'd seen her that his physical reaction to her had been a fluke. It wasn't. He'd opened the door to her office and raw longing had jolted him. She wore soft, flowing pants and a royal blue cashmere sweater, neither of which emphasized her curves, yet he knew they were there. The neck to her sweater dipped down in a vee, revealing a hint of the shadowed valley between her breasts where his eyes kept wandering. Her skin had a warm glow—she was amber all over from her hair to her eyes to her skin. It made him want to taste her so badly, he ached. She turned away from the window, her eyes catching his.

"I've visited a few times since Cam moved here, but I'm not sure I'll ever get used to seeing eagles almost every day," she said.

He had to force his mind to focus and not stare at her delectable mouth—lush and pink and so damn tempting with her dimple making occasional appearances. "I haven't," he finally replied. He was relieved when their waiter came to the table to take their order.

He'd obediently taken her to where Joan had made reservations at the Boathouse Café. The Boathouse was a local favorite. Once upon a time, it had been a standard diner, but the new owners had updated the classic diner look with polished mahogany tables, a bar with an extensive wine collection displayed on mahogany shelving with mirrors behind and copper cookware hanging above the open kitchen grill. The restaurant sat on a bluff overlooking Kachemak Bay, offering a close-up view of the glorious bay and mountains on the far side. He quickly ordered the halibut tacos and waited while Ivy asked a few questions of the waiter and eventually ordered the same dish.

After the waiter left with their menus, she looked over at him. "I've never had halibut tacos, so I had to try them."

"They're not quite like the usual tacos, but they're delicious. It's a good choice."

She took a sip of coffee and nodded. When he realized

she seemed to be waiting for him to speak next, he latched onto the only topic he could think of, seeing as he didn't seem too capable of casual conversation with Ivy. He was burning up with questions about her, so he talked about work instead. "I suppose we could talk about some of our projects."

She nodded, her amber eyes lighting up. "I'd love that. Between leaving the university and moving here, I haven't been able to dig into any research for over a month. I'd love to hear what you're doing and what I might be working on."

"Perfect. As you know, our main focus is developing clean, sustainable and affordable energy. There's plenty of wind and solar out there, along with the whole fuel cell idea. My concern has been much of what we have on the market now isn't cost-effective for the average homeowner, or business, looking to move in that direction, not to mention that roofs covered in panels and giant wind turbines aren't the most attractive. Off the Grid has three main projects we're focused on now. One is optimizing the capacity of solar panels to capture solar energy more efficiently, so panels can be smaller. Another is focusing on the wind issue. Wind turbines are fantastic, but they're huge. We're trying to create much smaller ones, so small they might look decorative in someone's yard. The other project is my baby—it's creating batteries that discharge and recycle all the energy they use in a form that's instantly reusable. The idea is to have no waste, whether it be through gas, heat, or other. My hope is these batteries will be used for anything from cars to appliances. I have some other ideas on my radar, but we try not to get stretched too thin. I was hoping to put you in the lead on the recycled energy project. I read your work on extending battery life for rockets and noticed you made some strides in getting the battery output to cycle back into the batteries themselves. Your ideas were solid, but you didn't get to keep going because—shocker—

they chopped the funding. That's an overview, but tell me what you think."

She stared back at him, her eyes wide and alive. A smile slowly spread across her face, bringing out her tempting dimple. He literally had to tell his body to calm down when he felt himself hardening just at the look on her face. *She isn't excited about anything to do with sex, man. This is all intellectual. Keep it that way.* Problem was, intellectual passion was the only passion he allowed himself. Adding her shared intellectual excitement to the equation of his attraction to her only made it multiply again and again.

"Oh this is awesome! Really? I can't believe this! The battery project was one of my favorites, and I was so bummed when they cut the funds for it."

"Unfortunately, funding for research is often the first to go. That's one of the reasons I decided to found Off the Grid. It's easier to raise money and reinvest the profits than it is to jump through the hoops for university funding. We have some grants, both government and university, that supplement, but we can survive without them."

Conversation carried on with Ivy peppering him with questions about the project—every question clearly demonstrating her thorough grounding in the topic. She didn't pause until their food arrived. By the time they left, he was buzzing, inside and out. The problem he'd convinced himself was nothing more than a passing issue—the electric physical attraction he felt toward Ivy—was turning out to be far more formidable than he'd anticipated. He walked beside her out to his SUV—matte black and decked out with every top-end detail available—and found his hand resting on the curve of her low back. He hadn't even realized he was touching her, it simply happened. He tried to tell himself he had to take his hand away, but he couldn't seem to do it. That small point of connection reverberated through his body, and he ached for more.

When they reached his SUV, he made sure she was situated in the passenger seat and turned away swiftly. He needed to get a handle on the lust searing through his body and fast. He managed small talk on the way back to the office by asking her about her move and how she was settling in. He noticed a subtle tension whenever he asked about her work at her last position. Her answers were clear, but he sensed a wariness and couldn't help but wonder what lay behind it.

They walked into the office with him breathing a sigh of relief that he'd gotten through lunch and kept his body under control. Again, his hands itched to touch her, but he managed not to, making it all the way to her office without slipping up. He stepped inside the door to her office. She was asking him something about reviewing the work on the project they'd discussed, but he barely heard her. She stopped just in front of him and shrugged her coat off. When she looked up, her cognac gaze locked with his, and he lost his mind. Without a thought passing through his brain, he took a step and lifted his hand, tracing it along the edge of her hair, which felt like silk as it slid through his fingers. The knot atop her head unraveled, her hair tumbling loose around her shoulders. Before he knew it, he'd dipped his head because he simply had to have a taste of her luscious lips. Her breath drew in sharply, the sound filtering into his awareness. He froze, suddenly aware he was about to cross a boundary he needed to keep in place. He couldn't quite bring himself to move though. They stood there, the soft sound of their breath rising and falling. Desire shimmered around them, the air alive with its weight.

He told himself he shouldn't, but his body was winning the battle and was listening only to the desire vibrating in an electric arc between them. He closed the whisper of space between their lips, bringing his to hers. Her mouth was pure heaven, her lips soft and full. A shock scored through him, the simple point of connection so loaded, he reeled internally. She tensed for a second and then sighed. He was lost. He stepped closer and angled his head to the side, diving into the temptation of her mouth. He tangled his hand in her hair and swept his tongue into her mouth, his body reveling in her instant response. Distantly, he heard footsteps coming down the hallway, a soft echo on the tiled floor. It took another second for awareness to nudge his body out of its raw drive. He tore his lips free.

Ivy's amber eyes stared back at him, wide and hazy with desire. He was rock hard with need and had to scramble for purchase in his mind to force himself to take a step back. The footsteps stopped before they reached Ivy's office. The sound of a door opening and closing came next. Owen couldn't look away from Ivy. He was rocked to his core. He didn't lose control. Ever. Until now.

CHAPTER 3

Ivy stood there, staring into Owen's eyes and frantically tried to collect herself. She was flushed inside and out, and her lips tingled from where his had been. Owen's eyes shuttered and he took a step back.

"Sorry about that. Not so sure what I was thinking." His words were clipped and icy.

The man who'd offered only glimpses of a warm side went cold and distant. Fortunately or unfortunately—Ivy wasn't sure which—Joan walked briskly into her office right then.

Her gaze landed on Owen. "Did you forget you scheduled a planning meeting for the battery project? Derek and Jana asked me where you were."

Owen gave his head a little shake. "Right. Headed that way in a few." He glanced to Ivy, his expression cold and distant and his eyes shuttered. "Joan will walk you to the conference room. I'll be there shortly." He spun on his heel and quickly departed her office, the door to his office closing with force.

Joan's warm brown eyes swung to Ivy. "Don't mind

Owen. He can be distant sometimes. No matter how many times I tell him it would help if he lightened up, he still hasn't figured it out. Trust me, I've known him for years. He's nicer than he seems at first."

Ivy nodded, still trying to slow her pulse and get a handle on her body's deep reaction to Owen's kiss. She tried to think of something to say, something to focus on other than Owen. "Is your daughter okay? Owen said she had a fever."

Joan nodded. "Katie's got a fever all right, but it's not too bad. We started her in swimming lessons this year, and she keeps getting ear infections. Along with those come fevers sometimes. She's napping in my office for the afternoon. Come on, I'll walk you to the conference room. This project will be yours if you can get Owen to let go a little." While Ivy wondered what that might mean, Joan winked and hooked her hand through Ivy's elbow, guiding her into the hallway.

Ivy felt rather short beside Joan because Joan was so tall. She had to be close to six feet with a thin frame. With her wide brown eyes and dark hair to match, Joan had a warm, practical beauty. She wore jeans and cowboy boots with a bright blue sweater that hung loosely over her lanky frame. Ivy had to walk quickly to keep up with Joan's stride, pondering Joan's comment about Owen's tendency to come across as distant as they walked. Ivy couldn't help but wonder what Joan would think if she knew Owen had kissed Ivy.

Ivy gave herself a mental shake. She could *not* let that kiss get to her. She wanted this job and didn't want to blow it by crossing lines with her boss. For crying out loud, she had to leave her last job because of a foolish, powerful man who she hadn't the least interest in. She definitely didn't like to find herself facing a genuine attraction to her new boss. The only thing helping her stay sane was the knowledge she hadn't initiated that kiss. That was all on him. Of course, the second his lips landed on hers, she'd lost all ability to think. She forced her mind onto batteries, that's right, batteries. Nothing sexy about them—she'd do what she did best and focus on her work. She was confident she'd get accustomed to being around Owen and this incredibly inconvenient attraction would fizzle out.

Hours later, Ivy walked into the late afternoon sunshine, pausing beside her car and taking in a gulp of the crisp winter air. Off the Grid was tucked in the hillside above Diamond Creek with its parking lot overlooking Kachemak Bay. At the moment, sunlight fell in a glittering path on the water. A light gust of wind sent a welcoming chill through her. The rest of her day had calmed her worries about Owen. Oh sure, there was that electric spark whenever they looked at each other, but as long as she managed to keep some distance between them, she could actually function. Once she'd had a chance to immerse her brain in her work, her body's haywire reaction to Owen eased. It helped that he ended up seated at the far end of the table away from her in the conference room. She left the meeting with a clear idea of where to start tomorrow, as far as what she'd be doing, and with a sense she could get a handle on her attraction to Owen.

As she drove away in her compact car, she couldn't help but wonder if he felt the same intensity between them. *Don't go there. Don't even go there. It's nothing more than a passing attraction.* She fervently hoped that to be true. She'd spent all of her adult life focused on her intellectual world. When her oldest brother died in a car accident a few years ago, she'd been devastated right alongside her parents and Cam. She'd taken a semester off from her doctoral program to be with them. Her parents had each other and had made it out from the worst of their grief. Cam, who'd been so close to Eric, had been knocked down hard, but he'd crawled out to the other side, in large part because he'd found his way to Alaska and found a life here with Ginger.

After Ivy had grieved the loss of Eric and tried to help patch up her family, she'd turned her focus even more intently onto academics. What interested her was putting her brain to work, not the vagaries of physical attraction. That's what had been so shocking about what happened at the university. She'd been thrilled beyond thrilled with Dr. Parkhurst's attention to her research during her doctoral program. His support had propelled her into her dream job as a researcher on the faculty at a nationally renowned engineering program. She'd been flying high and felt like she'd been granted a small blessing on the heels of the pain her family had gone through after Eric died. Her euphoria had been short lived. Within a few months, she'd been facing the brutal choice of whether to stay or go with the knowledge that she would all but blackball herself from academia if she left a faculty position that quickly. The decision ended up being made for her.

Just thinking about it now, she blinked back the tears that came on the heels of bitterness. She left the job of her dreams because she'd been politely asked to do so. Not because she did anything wrong, but because the chair of the engineering department where she worked had persistently pursued her to the point of harassment. Dr. Parkhurst had chaired the engineering department for almost twenty years and brought in gobs of grant funding with his outsize presence and alleged expertise. Ivy had the misfortune of being his latest sexual pursuit. Just thinking about him made her shudder. Not once, ever, had she looked at him in any way other than professionally. Not once had there been a hint of impropriety on her part. The human resources team was kind and polite, but they made it clear she might be better off if she cut her losses and left. Still, she wasn't giving up on her fight against Dr. Parkhurst and had filed a formal complaint, but she could hardly work under the hostile conditions once she turned him down—again and again and again.

Here she was now, walking into a new position at a world-renowned engineering firm and this time she was so attracted to her boss, she could barely think. To the point, thinking of Owen just now sent a wash of heat through her and she clenched her thighs. She had better get a handle on this and fast, or she'd be in trouble.

AT THE SOUND OF A KNOCK, Owen spun on the stool by his worktable. When he saw Derek Bridges through the glass door to his office, he gestured for him to come in. Derek stepped through the door and strode to the opposite side of the table. Hooking his booted foot around another stool, Derek sat down and eyed Owen. "You like the new engineer," he said by way of greeting.

Derek was a friend from United Tech and had joined at Off the Grid when Owen decided to move the business to Alaska. He was currently in charge of the wind turbine projects and was Owen's most trusted researcher. They'd worked together on projects at United Tech. Derek was blunt and direct about anything and everything, so Owen knew he could count on him to keep things on the level. He also didn't shy away from making pointed observations, hence his opening salvo about Ivy.

Owen tapped save on the digital diagram he'd been reviewing and looked over at Derek. He'd hoped no one would notice his reaction to Ivy, but he should've known Derek would. "I hired her. Of course I like her. She's brilliant and has the background for what we need," he said with a shrug, aiming for casual in his reply.

Derek ran a hand through his dark blonde hair, his

brown eyes narrowing. "Of course you'd say that. That's not what I meant. You *like* her."

Owen wasn't up for bantering about Ivy, most certainly not about the raging lust she elicited. He was still mentally bashing himself for losing his mind and kissing her. He returned Derek's narrowed stare. "I don't know what your point is, but I'd rather discuss the latest data from your project."

Derek held his gaze for another beat and then shrugged. He might be observant and blunt, but he wasn't one to push on personal issues. Given Owen's tendency to prefer to keep even his friends at a comfortable distance that was one reason Derek was such a good and trusted friend. He respected the distance Owen set with everyone. Oddly enough, his respect brought him closer to Owen. Outside of Joan, if there was a friend and colleague Owen would turn to in times of trouble, it was Derek.

Derek spun one of the computer screens on the table in his direction and tapped a few icons on the screen. "Okay, here's what we're looking at." Within seconds, they were immersed in a review of data and assessing the implications of a few tweaks Derek and his team had made to an innovative wind capture system.

Hours later, it was dark outside and Owen stood up from his worktable and strode to the windows. Derek had left over an hour ago. Owen figured most of the building was empty now. He was almost always the last person to leave and tended to work as late as midnight some nights. Derek occasionally teased that Owen should've put a bed in his office. Owen had a house on the massive property he'd purchased for Off the Grid. He owned over three hundred acres on the outskirts of Diamond Creek. Aside from the company offices, he'd built his dream home just down the road—a fully self-sustaining home with the same breathtaking views offered at the office. The rest of the property was nothing but wilderness and trails.

He stared out into the night sky. The moon was a curved sliver above the mountains, their snow-capped peaks barely visible in the darkness. He considered Derek's comment about Ivy. Owen had gone out of his way to keep his distance from Ivy during the meeting in the conference room. He'd invited Derek to the meeting since Derek had his fingers all over the battery project as well, although of late he'd moved his attention elsewhere at Owen's request. Problem was, even with the length of the conference room table separating him from Ivy and plenty of active discussion on topics that usually held his attention, Owen's body hummed at the feel of Ivy's presence across the room.

To say Owen wasn't interested in a relationship was an understatement. He emphatically didn't ever want to experience the emotionally brutal toll of losing someone he loved. The loss of his parents had taught him far more than he'd ever wanted to know about how capricious life could be. To this day, that loss echoed. He'd made a choice to control what he could in his life, and that included keeping people at a distance. He dated and kept things clearly casual. He was so committed to casual that he pointedly didn't get involved with anyone local. Diamond Creek was too small, and he didn't want to run the risk of unintentionally leading someone on. He hadn't found this to be limiting, or even difficult. When he looked back, he hadn't made a conscious decision at first. He was barely nineteen when his parents died. Over the years though, the choice had become purposeful. His intellectual pursuits fulfilled him on many levels. He had a small circle of friends he kept close and that was enough. He'd yet to meet a woman who even gave him pause.

Ivy sent him spinning sideways inside. It wasn't simply the raw physical pull he felt for her. If it was just that, he could easily manage the situation. It was the pure magnetic connection, plus the fact that she stepped onto the intellectual field with him and met him on equal terms with as much passion as anyone he'd ever seen. He'd heard as such about her before her resume had landed in his inbox. It had never crossed his mind he might be so attracted to a woman, he'd lose focus at work. His mind replayed the memory of how her lips felt under his, his body instantly tightening. With a muttered curse, he spun away from the windows and grabbed his jacket.

Within moments, he walked into his house. He turned up the heat and started a fire in the soapstone fireplace. Even though he knew intellectually that wood fires weren't the most efficient, he loved the scent and feel of one. He'd gone with soapstone because it retained heat for hours and hours. The soapstone chimney went straight up through the center of the roof in his octagonal home. The stone would radiate heat throughout the cold night and still be warm to the touch in the morning.

Once a fire was crackling in the fireplace, Owen strode to the kitchen. The octagonal home offered a wide-open layout on the main floor. The kitchen and a dining area occupied one side of the space with the fireplace, open to both sides of the area, serving as a natural divider. The living room area, if one wanted to call it that, was to the other side with a large, comfortable sectional and several chairs with small tables scattered throughout. A bathroom was off the kitchen, the only room on the main floor that had walls and a door. A master bedroom and bath occupied the entire upper floor, reached by a spiral staircase tucked against the wall. Another staircase led downstairs, which contained a workout room, laundry, a bathroom and two more bedrooms, both of which had gone unused since he'd built the home. He opened his refrigerator to find hardly anything in there. His eyes landed on a casserole dish with a note on it.

He snagged the note to find his name written in Joan's tidy handwriting. *Just so you don't starve.* She'd added a smiley face at the bottom. He couldn't help but smile. Joan, her husband Reggie, and their daughter were the closest thing he had to family. Joan and Reggie were roughly ten years older than him and had taken him under their wing after his parents died. Their ten-year old daughter, Katie, was named after his mother. To this day, Joan said his mother had been like a mother to her, giving her a job when she was fresh out of college and casting about in her life.

He pulled out the casserole and looked under the cover to find some kind of creamy pasta dish. With full faith in Joan's cooking, he put the casserole in the oven and set the timer. He immediately carted his laptop over to the couch and tried to return to work while he waited. His focus was so scattered he found himself bouncing between thoughts of Ivy—her cognac eyes behind her glasses, the delectable dimple at the corner of her mouth, and her tempting curves.

He woke the following morning on the couch, irritable from the moment he opened his eyes. His neck was sore from an odd angle, his clothes were rumpled, and he'd notched maybe three hours of sleep.

All because of Ivy.

CHAPTER 4

"Well, hey George," Ivy said, looking down at the gray rabbit who'd just bounced into her lap.

George's solemn blue eyes studied her for a moment before he leaned his head into her hand. She stroked his soft fur and looked up from where she was sitting at the kitchen table in Ginger and Cam's house. Ginger was at the stove, busy stirring the stir-fry she was making for dinner.

"How long have you had George?" Ivy asked.

Ginger's glossy dark hair swung in its ponytail when she glanced over her shoulder. Her blue eyes crinkled at the corners with her smile when she saw George on Ivy's lap. "About four years. He's spoiled rotten, and I love him to pieces," Ginger declared as she turned back to the pan on the stove. She gave the vegetables and chicken another stir and then turned off the burner.

"Cam even loves him now," Ginger said as she sat down across from Ivy.

Ivy grinned as she stroked George's soft fur. "I've noticed." She looked up at Ginger. "I'm so glad Cam found you," she said, suddenly overcome with how happy she was to know Cam had Ginger now. In the aftermath of their brother's death, Cam had been hit hard. He and Eric had competed on the professional ski circuit together for most of their lives. Eric had been driving in the car accident that killed him. He hadn't bothered with his seatbelt and had been thrown from the vehicle. Cam, always the more practical of her two brothers, had been wearing his seatbelt. He'd come away with minor injuries and crushing grief. Only after he took a job at Last Frontier Lodge here in Diamond Creek and found Ginger had he discovered joy again. Ivy adored Cam and had worried about him so much after Eric died.

Bold, bright and with a sly sense of humor, Ginger was the perfect match for Cam. Ivy considered it a total bonus that she and Ginger had become fast friends and sisters. Ginger caught her eyes and reached over to squeeze her hand. "I'm glad I found him too. I'm not as sentimental as you, but I have my moments."

Ivy laughed softly and watched as George bounded from her lap to Ginger's in one smooth leap.

"It's been almost a week now. How are you feeling about your job?" Ginger asked.

Owen flashed through Ivy's mind, heat rolling through her at the mere thought of his startlingly bright blue eyes, jet-black hair and muscled body. The moment she batted that thought away, she thought of his intellectual drive. That was the problem. She figured she could find a way to move past her burning attraction for him, even if it was so hot it almost scalded her. Yet, she didn't know how to beat that back when she also felt such an affinity for his thinking. She'd spent her entire academic career working on the type of projects Off the Grid was researching and building. She loved her work, down to her bones. It wasn't easy to find people who shared her passion, and Owen did.

Ginger cleared her throat, prompting Ivy to realize she'd been sitting there silent, meandering off on another tangent in her mind and body about Owen. She gave herself a shake and met Ginger's eyes. "It's good." Her reply was entirely true. Her job was good, so good it terrified her. She'd been so focused on succeeding in the world of academia, she had closed herself off from the possible joy of working on the other side of research. In the single week she'd been at Off the Grid, she'd almost clapped so many times when she realized her research had the possibility to become actual products.

"What's Owen Manning like?" Ginger asked.

Ivy felt her cheeks heat, but she ignored it. "He's driven, and he's brilliant," she replied, trying to stick to the work details.

Ginger rolled her eyes. "Well, duh. You told us that before you even met him. The man is a bit of a mystery around here. He moved Off the Grid here last year, built that amazing compound up on the hill and pretty much stays there. Cam knows him a bit because he likes to ski and goes to the lodge a lot, but other than that, he's managed to keep to himself around here. That's no easy task. I met Joan, his HR person. She's awesome. Her daughter's cute as a button. Anyway, he'd probably hate to hear it, but there's plenty of gossip about him. You can't be all sexy and mysterious in Diamond Creek without making people curious. It doesn't hurt that he's obviously loaded. Everyone who works there so far came with him, so it's all hush-hush. I can't help but wonder. What's he like personally?"

Ivy's mind flashed to the feel of his lips against hers. She forced her thoughts away from that, and they immediately went to the many tiny moments she'd observed him in the week she'd been at Off the Grid. His presence was almost overwhelming anytime she was near him, but she'd learned once she was focused on the details of work, she could tolerate it. She'd quickly come to admire the hell out of him. He was driven and brilliant, but he lacked the arrogance that was so often part and parcel of men high on the ladder in the engineering world. He clearly had his finger on the pulse of everything happening at Off the Grid, but he had no problem letting go of control. He listened to any and all feedback and appeared to fully trust those who worked for him. She sensed his expectation was for her to take over the battery projects, but he seemed to be making sure she was ready for him to step back. That elated and terrified her at once.

Ginger cleared her throat again. When Ivy caught her eyes, the flush that had started to fade raced up her cheeks again. Ginger smiled slowly. "Oh I get it. You think he's hot." She lifted a shoulder in a shrug. "That's a plain fact, so no need to be embarrassed. If you ask me, it's good. You're so brainy, you intimidate me sometimes. Nice to know you're human," she said wryly.

Ivy stared at Ginger, trying to will her blush away and failing completely. She finally shook her head. "Fine. He's hot. I'll get over it. It's just kind of inconvenient, especially after what went down with Dr. Parkhurst. I've never in my life even noticed someone I work with, and I had to leave a job because of an asshole. I guess I didn't expect to notice Owen, so it's weird. I'm sure it'll pass."

Ginger's gaze sobered, her eyes narrowing. "You did absolutely nothing wrong at your old job! Dr. Parkhurst is a creeper. The worst kind. How many harassment complaints were filed on him? Something like ten, or that's what I heard. It's better you left that university job anyway. You would've been trapped kissing ass for years to get any recognition. At Off the Grid, you can do everything you want without all that bullshit. Plus, having the hots for your totally sexy boss in a private company is different. Not to mention, you don't technically work for him. Remember? I helped you with all the hiring paperwork. He has you set up as a private contractor with buy in to all the benefits. It's smart for him and smart for you. Normally, I'd say that wasn't a good option, but Off the Grid is incredibly generous with the benefit options, so it's like all the pluses of technically working for them with more freedom. So if you look at it that way..." Ginger trailed off with a wink.

Ivy stared at Ginger, her mouth dropping open at Ginger's audaciousness. "Are you crazy? I can't think about him like that."

Ginger was unabashed and shrugged. "Honey, you can think whatever you want. I was just pointing out you didn't need to let the whole 'job' thing get in the way."

Ivy shook her head forcefully. "It's not about technicalities. This job is everything I ever wanted. I don't want to be stupid and mess it up."

Ginger's grin faded. "Right. There is that. Well, I'm sure you'll settle in and stop drooling over him."

The front door opened and Cam stepped through. Ivy watched as George bounced off Ginger's lap and straight to Cam's feet. Ginger caught Ivy's eye. "George gets the first hello."

Cam straightened from petting George and looked over into the kitchen. "Only because he's so fast." Cam toed off his boots and walked into the kitchen.

The home he shared with Ginger was on a bluff by Kachemak Bay. The downstairs was comprised of a living room with a kitchen to the side through an archway with a guest bedroom, a small bathroom and laundry room to the other side. A wall of windows afforded a clear view of the rocky beach and bay. Cam plunked down at the table. "It smells amazing. What's for dinner?" He leaned over and dropped a kiss on Ginger's cheek, lingering for a second.

"Chicken and veggie stir fry," Ginger replied. "Ivy did the chopping and I cooked."

Cam glanced to Ivy, his amber eyes meeting hers with a gleam. "Perfect. I'm starving. How was your day?"

"Good."

"Just good?"

Ivy glanced sideways at Ginger, praying she wasn't in the mood to tease about Owen. Ginger was standing up from the table, so Ivy breathed a mental sigh of relief. She was quite close to her brother, but she generally didn't discuss romance in her life with him. The truth was there'd never been any romance to discuss. "Yup. Just good. I'm settling in, getting to know the lay of the land at Off the Grid and staying busy. How about you?"

Cam leaned back in his chair and ran a hand through his amber hair. She shared his coloring, although her hair and eyes were a tad bit darker. "I'm exhausted. We had ski clinic today, which is fun, but we've got a rowdy group this winter. Another skier got lost on the cross-country trails, so Gage and I spent the afternoon skiing all over the place up there. Doesn't seem to matter how well we mark the trails and how many liability releases we make people sign about staying on trail, there's someone every week who takes off on their own."

Ginger spoke from the counter where she was serving food onto plates for them. "Since you're not saying it, I'm assuming you found whoever got lost." She turned with two plates in her hands and set them down in front of Ivy and Cam. "He always does this. Tells me stories about people getting lost and doesn't bother to mention if they're okay."

Cam chuckled. "Yeah, we found the guy. No shocker, but it was a twenty-year old kid. He fell in the ravine by the stream that cuts through the trail section. He's damn lucky he wore a bright jacket. He twisted his knee, so he's got some nasty bruising and won't be skiing for a few days. His girlfriend had enough sense to stay on the trail, so we found out pretty quick he'd gotten lost."

Conversation moved on. The longer she was in Diamond Creek, the more relaxed Ivy became. After dinner, they spread out in the living room. Ivy had lived on her own ever since she'd started graduate school. That meant long nights researching and writing papers by herself. Though she'd grown up in a close family, she hadn't realized how much she missed evenings with others until she came to stay with Cam and Ginger. They'd insisted it was a waste of time for her to try to find her own place this time of year. With spring on the way soon, Ginger had explained any rentals would be taken over for the tourist season. For now, Ivy planned to stay with them through next winter and assess what to do then.

Hours later, she lay in bed, trying and failing to keep her mind from chewing on Ginger's comment about how she was technically an independent contractor for Owen. Her forbidden and overpowering attraction to Owen didn't seem so forbidden in that light. She finally fell into a fitful sleep, waking before the sun came up, her mind muddled and her body out of sorts due to her restless sleep.

All because of Owen.

CHAPTER 5

Owen leaned forward, curling into a turn on the ski slope. He savored the rush of flying down the mountain. The icy air energized him as he angled back and forth down the steep slope, coming to a swirling stop at the base with snow flying in an arc around him. He closed his eyes and gulped in a breath. Opening his eyes again, he glanced up the slope, which was dotted with bright colors— the jackets of skiers decorating the snowy white expanse. On the heels of another breath, he pushed off on his skis again, aiming straight for the lift. He spent most of his weekends at Last Frontier Lodge when he wasn't working. Skiing was pure joy for him—between the exhilaration of speed, the physical escape, and the sheer beauty of skiing in Alaska, there wasn't much else that cleared his mind the way skiing did.

He skied off the lift at the top of the advanced slopes and paused. For the moment, he was alone up here, high in the crisp mountain air. He slowly circled, surveying the view. Diamond Creek's location on Kachemak Bay in Alaska offered breathtaking scenery with the mountains surrounding the town and the bay spilling out in view. Tourists flocked here for good reason, and the community catered to them. The ski lodge was situated above Diamond Creek, offering a three hundred and sixty degree view of the area. Not too far in the distance, Off the Grid was visible, tucked into the trees on the hillside.

Two volcanoes were visible with Mount Augustine standing tall in the waters of Cook Inlet at the entrance to Kachemak Bay and Mount Illiamna further away—both snow covered. Owen turned to face the entrances to the slopes and took a deep breath of the spruce scented air. It was late February with spring not technically far away. Alaskan winters were long though, and the snow would cling until as late as May. When Owen decided to move to Alaska, the long winters were a draw for more than one reason. With skiing one of the only activities that took his mind off work, he'd been thrilled with the idea of skiing for six months or more every year. In addition, Alaska seasons offered the harsh conditions he wanted to test the products Off the Grid created. Running hypothetical models of how a wind powered furnace would hold up in a long winter were never as effective as actual tests under true conditions.

The ski lift rounded the top of the slope and slowed to drop off a single skier. Owen glanced over to see Cam Nash skiing off the lift in his direction. The sight of Ivy's brother immediately conjured her in his mind—yet again, the searing memory of her lips under his sent a hot jolt through him. He didn't realize he was actually shaking his head until Cam skied to his side.

"Unhappy to see me?" Cam asked with a grin.

Owen caught himself and managed a chuckle. "Nah." Uncertain what to say about why he was shaking his head, he elected not to bother trying to explain. He couldn't exactly consider the truth, which was that Ivy, who happened to be Cam's sister, had him nearly tied up in knots every time he thought about her. He didn't know Cam well enough to know if he'd care about something like that, yet Owen's reticence also came from his preference to keep his private life private. That was much easier to do when he wasn't dealing with his scorching attraction to Ivy and wrestling with her emotional pull on him.

Cam eased to a stop beside him, leaning on one of his ski poles. As Owen met his eyes, he realized Ivy and Cam shared the same coloring. He hadn't really considered it, nor could he have said he ever noticed Cam's eyes before. But right now, he saw they were a slightly lighter shade of amber than Ivy's. Cam scanned the area before his gaze landed on Owen again. "I'm guessing you put two and two together and figured out my sister's working with you now," Cam said.

Owen nodded and willed his mind to behave and not think about Ivy in any way other than the abstract. His mind instantly disobeyed, this time recalling the brief feel of her soft curves against his body in that moment of madness when he kissed her. He skipped tracks to the moment during a meeting the other day when she was reviewing data on the battery project with a few team members. Her silky amber hair had fallen loose from its knot, and he'd wanted to run his fingers through it. He started to shake his head again when he caught himself, realizing Cam would think he was half-crazy if he kept randomly shaking his head. He swallowed and met Cam's eyes. "When she mentioned she had family here, I put it together. Gotta say, you two definitely went in different directions."

Cam flashed a grin. "Oh yeah. Ivy's been the smartest member of the family since the day she was born. I was already competing on the backcountry circuit by the time I was in high school. If I ever had the potential to be as brilliant as her, I wasted it on the slopes."

Cam's pride in Ivy was so obvious, it gave Owen's heart

a squeeze. He couldn't resist the pull of his curiosity about Ivy's family. "I'd say you're a genius in your own field. You didn't get to be world famous in backcountry skiing for nothing. I never did ask, but how'd you get started competing?"

Cam's expression sobered as he looked out toward the bay. "Our older brother started first, and I followed in his footsteps. Before I knew it, that's all we did. It was fun, but the schedule and travel were hard after a while." He slowly turned back to Owen. "Skiing's a huge part of my life and I love it, but I'm happier here in Diamond Creek than I ever was chasing medals."

Owen sensed he was missing something important, but he wasn't sure what. He asked the natural question that came to mind next. "Is your brother still competing?"

Pain flashed in Cam's eyes before he took a deep breath. "Eric died in a car accident. I never competed again after that."

"Damn. I'm sorry, Cam. I had no idea." Owen knew all too well the pain of a loss like that, so he felt genuinely bad about stumbling into the topic.

Cam shook his head. "It's okay. No way you could've known. For a long time, I didn't think I'd know I was over Eric's death until I competed again, but turned out all I needed to do was remember how much I loved to ski. Ivy held our family together afterwards. She's not just an engineer, she's got a big heart. Before you know it, she'll be taking care of everyone at your office," he said with a chuckle.

His curiosity about Ivy grew by leaps and bounds with the little windows into her personality Cam was providing. He managed to stay focused on the actual conversation. "Well, I'm sorry to hear about your brother, but it sounds like you've found a good place. Diamond Creek's about as good as it gets as far as I'm concerned, so I see why you love it here."

Cam shrugged. "Oh, it's gorgeous and the skiing's amazing, but that's not what made me stay. It's Ginger and everyone else here. My family was always close, but with the traveling I did, I never got to enjoy it much. Between Ginger and everyone here at the lodge, it's like a second family. Our parents come up all the time now too. I doubt they'd retire here because they want to be somewhere warm. I'm damn happy Off the Grid brought Ivy here. She's not happy if she can't spin the wheels in her engineering brain, so when I heard she applied at your business, I figured it'd be a good fit for her. Never did think the whole academic world suited her personality. Not to mention the asshole who chased her out of her last position."

"What do you mean?" Owen asked, a flash of anger mingling with his curiosity. He didn't even know what he was angry about, but Cam's tone indicated someone had treated Ivy badly. He didn't like that, not one bit.

Cam shook his head, a look of disgust passing over his face. "She'll probably never mention it, but the chair at her department took a shine to her and not the good kind. Old creeper if you ask me. I told her to get the hell out of there. He made her life miserable. She looks better than she has in over a year now that she's out of there."

Owen's mind spun with questions, while anger simmered inside. No woman deserved that kind of bullshit, but it was common in the world of academia. The 'old creepers' Cam described often held positions of power on faculties and wielded it as they chose. Hearing that was what pushed Ivy out infuriated him. He was beyond thrilled to have her and the brilliance she brought with her at Off the Grid, and he truly believed it would have been wasted in a university setting, but it made him sick to learn what prompted her to make a change.

"I'd like to say that surprises me, but it's all too common in that world," he finally managed. "We're happy to have her at Off the Grid, so it's a win for me."

Somehow he managed to get the conversation onto more casual terrain over the next few minutes. He was pondering which slope to ski down when Cam caught his eye as the ski lift rolled toward them again. "Race you down," Cam said with a grin.

"You're on!"

Just like that, they pushed off in unison toward the steepest slope. Owen couldn't claim to have the depth of experience Cam did from his days of competition, but he loved to let his skis take over and fly down the slope. This wasn't their first impromptu race. By the time they spun to a stop, his eyes were watering from the icy wind. Snow spun in a wild arc around them. He glanced over to find Cam laughing.

"Damn. Not sure I could tell which one of us made it here first," Cam said once he stopped laughing.

Gage Hamilton slid to a stop on his skis beside Cam, his eyes bouncing between them. "Pretty sure it was Owen," he said with a nod in Owen's direction.

Cam shrugged. "If you say so."

Gage laughed. "Couldn't actually tell myself. All I know is you always want to beat me, but you don't seem to care with anyone else."

Cam chuckled. "Maybe so."

Gage caught Owen's gaze. "How's it going today?"

"Any day I'm skiing for a few hours is a good day."

Owen mostly kept to himself, but he'd gotten to know Gage and Cam because of their presence at Last Frontier Lodge. Gage owned the lodge with his siblings, although he was the one who'd renovated the once boarded up lodge and brought it back to life as a world-class resort. Owen appreciated Gage. He was friendly and welcoming, but he let Owen keep his distance. He tended to be serious, but lightened up around his wife Marley and a few regulars at the lodge. Cam ran the ski programs for the lodge. When he wasn't working, Owen spent most of his free time at the lodge skiing, so he probably knew Gage and Cam better than most anyone outside of Off the Grid.

Gage flashed a grin. "Of course any day skiing's a good day. Have you had a chance to check out our new cross country trails?"

"You added more?" Owen asked, thinking that they already had over forty miles of trails.

Gage smiled sheepishly. "Can't help myself."

A voice called Cam's name, sending a prickle up Owen's spine. Without seeing her, he knew it was Ivy's voice and turned to see her skiing in their direction. This was a problem he hadn't considered. Actually, it was the lust pounding through him every time Ivy was near that was the problem. He should've expected to see her at the ski lodge because her brother worked here—the brother she'd made clear meant a lot to her. He'd have to find a way to keep his distance.

Ivy skied over, a wide smile on her face, her tempting dimple making him want to kiss her. Right here, right now where he absolutely shouldn't be thinking anything like that.

"Hey sis," Cam said with a grin. "You and Ginger have fun on the trails?"

"Of course! She's right behind me." Ivy glanced over her shoulder. "She stopped to talk to someone."

Cam chuckled. "She always stops to talk to someone. I swear every time we go somewhere, I figure I'd better plan an extra half hour just to give her time."

Ivy beamed at Cam. "Tease all you want. You love her and you know it."

Cam didn't miss a beat. "That I do." He nodded in

Owen's direction. "Gage claims Owen beat me down the mountain."

Ivy's gaze swung to him, her eyes widening slightly. She didn't appear to have noticed him until then. Her eyes bounced back to Cam, a sly smile stretching across her face. "Nice to know someone can beat you."

Owen couldn't help the heat that rose within at the sight of Ivy's smile. The effect she had on him was ridiculous. He shifted his shoulders, disconcerted by his reaction to her. He preferred to feel in control. With Ivy, well, he felt the opposite most of the time.

Cam chuckled and punched her lightly in the shoulder. He turned toward the sprawling deck behind the lodge. "Meet you inside for some food in a bit?"

Ivy nodded. "I'll go drag Ginger in."

Cam caught Owen's eyes. "How about you join us for a bit? Delia makes a killer hot cider."

"Have you had Delia's cider yet?" Gage asked.

"Can't say I have. I also don't know who Delia is."

"How did I miss that you've been skiing here since last winter and never once ate in the restaurant?" Gage asked. "Seriously, not because I'm trying to sell something—in fact, it's on me if you decide to stop in this afternoon—but you can't miss Delia's cider and cooking. She runs the restaurant..."

"And makes the lodge restaurant my absolute favorite place to eat!" Ivy added, nodding firmly.

"Right, that about says it," Gage finished.

Owen found himself sliding into a booth in the lodge restaurant a few minutes later. Truth was, he'd never even been past the reception area in the ski lodge. He glanced around the restaurant. A wall of windows offered a wide open view of the slopes and mountains surrounding the ski lodge. The restaurant had booths along the inside walls with tables in the center of the room. With exposed beams and hardwood floors, the restaurant felt like, well, a lodge. The décor was simple with crisp white tablecloths serving as a contrast to the wood surfaces, lending itself to a comfortable and homey space.

Somehow he'd ended up seated beside Ivy, which was an instantaneous combination of pleasure and pain. He was taut with need and fighting back a hard on, all because she happened to be sitting beside him. Cam sat across from him with his arm slung over the woman Owen presumed to be Ginger. Gage had tugged a chair up at the end of the booth and was talking with Don Peters whom Owen had met in passing. Just as Don turned away, Gage nudged Owen's shoulder. "You've met Don, right?"

Don's weathered face brightened with his smile. "Course he has. He helped me a few months ago when the damn lift broke up on the mountain."

"Delia is Don's daughter, the one who makes the amazing cider," Gage added.

Don chuckled. "If you haven't had that, you'd best try some." With a nod, he ambled away, pushing through the swinging door that led to the kitchen.

Owen couldn't say how, but he made it through the unexpectedly social afternoon without a hitch. It helped that everyone there was easy to be around, minus the constant delectable distraction of Ivy. Aside from that inconvenient challenge, she was pure joy to be around—warm and easy-going. He got to see a side of her he hadn't yet seen at work. Around her family and friends, the soft side Cam mentioned was quite evident. The cider was as delicious as promised, so delicious Owen asked if he'd be able to buy some to bring home.

Ginger's snappy blue eyes landed on him. "See! All you have to do is taste it and then you want more." She brushed a lock of her glossy dark hair out of her eyes. "Just have Harry get some for you."

Harry had waited on them and appeared to be spinning through the restaurant most of the time. Gage lifted a hand and waved Harry over, quickly asking him to get some bottled cider for Owen. After Harry left the booth, Ginger pinned him with her gaze again. "So Owen, you've been in Diamond Creek for over a year. What do you think?"

Owen had quickly noticed Ginger was direct, which he didn't mind because it saved him the trouble of wondering what she might be thinking. "I knew I wanted to move Off the Grid here before I made plans. I visited Alaska a few times when I was in grad school. I didn't get a chance to ski here because Last Frontier Lodge wasn't open, but I spent a weekend here and loved it. Still do."

Ginger nodded, her eyes thoughtful. It was no more than a blink, but he saw her eyes flick to Ivy and back to him. He couldn't help but wonder if she noticed how much he noticed Ivy. She didn't comment further and the conversation moved on. Owen could feel the warmth of Ivy beside him. With her thigh pressed against his, he had to fight the urge to touch her. He could feel the soft rise and fall of her breath, while lust tightened its grip on him. Every so often, he'd catch himself zoning out, losing sight of where they were. His hunger for her was a force of its own—one he couldn't control. Just now, she glanced up at him, her amber lashes framing her gorgeous cognac eyes behind her glasses. He had to curl his hands into fists to keep from touching her when what he wanted was to slide his hand into her silky hair and fit his mouth over hers. The need to let loose the reins of his control was so great, he almost forgot himself. With lust lashing at him and his cock rock-hard, Ginger said something, and he tore his eyes away.

Not much later, he pulled up at the office. The days were getting longer with the sun just starting its slide down the sky in the early evening. Owen needed to bury his mind in work. He was beyond distracted after a few hours in Ivy's company. He was also off kilter at how easily he'd settled into the afternoon with her family and friends. Outside of the small circle of friends who'd followed Off the Grid to Alaska, he hadn't allowed himself interactions like this afternoon. For years, he'd avoided such situations because he didn't want to miss what he'd lost. Though it had been just him and his parents growing up, they had a wide circle of friends who were often at the house. Casual evenings of banter and warmth filled his childhood memories. Oddly, today he'd had a few moments when he missed what he'd lost, but not the way he used to.

He'd spent so many years controlling the circumstances of his life that he hadn't allowed openings like this and didn't know what to make of it. He jogged into the building. Out of habit, he did a loop around the building, checking to make sure lights were out and computers powered down. They always were, but he'd developed the habit of checking. He sensed he did it as much for how rewarding it felt to know Off the Grid was a thriving research firm as he did to actually check on anything. On a Saturday evening, the office was close to empty until he turned down the hallway where his office was and found Derek with his eyes glued to a computer screen and a pot of coffee sitting on his desk.

Owen leaned in the doorway, bemused to realize Derek hadn't noticed his presence yet. After another moment, he cleared his throat, and Derek whipped his head around.

The second Derek saw Owen, he cracked a grin. "I was wondering where you were. You usually finish skiing earlier than this." Derek spun in his chair to face Owen. "What's up?"

Owen shrugged. "Just stopping by for a few hours. Thought I'd take a look at the changes Ivy suggested for the battery project and get started on some applications to lead the research on the federal energy efficiency initiative. You?"

Derek tapped his fingers on the edge of his worktable. "Finishing up on some data reports."

The sound of footsteps echoed in the tiled hallway. Derek arched a brow. "Bets on who that is?"

Owen rolled his eyes. "No clue, so I'm not about to bet."

"It's gotta be Ivy," Derek said with a slow grin.

Owen leaned his head out of Derek's office to discover Derek was right. Ivy was walking down the long hallway, her eyes on some papers in her hands. She was still wearing her fitted ski pants with a tank top hugging her chest and a sleek black ski jacket that hung open. Her hair was tied up in a knot with loose glossy amber curls escaping. His pulse lunged, and his body tightened. He was becoming familiar with the feeling she elicited in him, yet it remained unsettling in its power. With a forceful mental shake, he glanced back to Derek. "Good guess."

Derek chuckled and pushed his chair back as he stood. "I was about to head out anyway."

Ivy's footsteps reached Derek's doorway and stopped. "Oh! I didn't even hear you guys."

Derek grinned at her. "We're not that loud. What brings you here on a Saturday evening?"

"I wanted to do some more work on that data I was compiling yesterday. It's not too late, so..." Her words trailed off as she shrugged. A subtle wash of pink rose in her cheeks.

Owen managed a polite nod. "Looks like we're all thinking about data. I'll stay out of your way."

Well aware that Derek had already picked up on his attraction to Ivy despite his avoidance of the topic, Owen wanted to clear out of there before Derek noticed much more. Willing his body under control, Owen pushed his shoulder off the doorframe and gave a quick wave to them both before striding down the hallway to his office.

CHAPTER 6

$\mathcal{I}$vy had to force herself to hold still as Owen brushed past her. His eyes were trained on the floor. She looked back to Derek, fighting to keep from flushing. Owen's icy distance just now was disconcerting. It was bad enough she didn't know how to manage the humming in her body every time he was near, but he ran hot and cold, which confused her. Derek met her eyes, his mouth hooking in a rueful smile. She'd quickly come to notice Derek could read others easily. Whenever he was in team meetings, he deftly navigated when there were competing opinions, reading the room with ease. He was easy-going, warm and clearly respected by everyone at Off the Grid. Ivy hoped to get to know him a little better because she could use some guidance on how to find her footing here at Off the Grid. The environment was so unlike the academic world, which was guided by rigid structure and rules. She'd known the process for finding her place there—basically keep her head down and work her tail off without expecting much recognition for years.

Here at Off the Grid, everyone seemed to be on a level

playing field. Though it was clear Owen was in charge, he treated all staff with the same respect and consideration. He'd made it clear he expected her to take the lead on the battery project, yet she wasn't used to taking the lead on anything. She didn't question her intellectual heft in the area, but she was so used to working in the shadows, she didn't know quite what to do. She wanted to ask Owen for his feedback, but between his unexpected kiss, the desire she couldn't seem to banish no matter how hard she tried, and his aloofness, she didn't know what the hell to do.

She took a breath and met Derek's gaze with a shrug. She was considering her words when he spoke.

"Don't mind Owen. He takes a while to warm up," Derek said as he slid his laptop into a bag. He leaned his hips against the table. He proceeded to prove her quite right about how well he could read others. "I'm guessing this place is a far cry from your university position."

Ivy bit the inside of her cheek and nodded. "Oh yeah. It's great though. I love it, I really do. I'm just trying to figure things out."

"You're doing great. I read your research from back when you were in grad school, so I figured we got lucky when you applied for the position here. It's only been a week, and you've already made your mark on several projects." He paused as if he was considering his next words. "Owen doesn't ever get warm and fuzzy. It helps if you know a little bit about him. He's tight with Joan's family because they were there for him after his parents died. I didn't meet Owen until we were at United Tech together. If you think he's distant now, it was worse back then. According to Joan, he was devastated when his parents died and he's never been the same since."

Ivy's hand flew to her mouth. "Oh, that's so sad! How did they die?"

"Carbon monoxide poisoning. If you ever wondered

why Owen was so damn passionate about making sure everything we design has clean output, now you know."

Ivy's heart squeezed for Owen. She knew what it was like to lose someone you loved. Her family had staggered after her oldest brother Eric died. She tried to imagine losing both of her parents at once, the mere idea of it taking her breath away. She met Derek's kind brown eyes. "You mean they died at the same time?"

Derek nodded. "Yup. Joan said it was awful. She worked for Owen's mother at the time."

Ivy nodded slowly, still trying to absorb how painful such a loss must have been.

Derek continued. "If you're wondering why Owen keeps his distance, that's why. Kinda have to learn that's what you get with him. Thing is, he's one of the best guys I know. Don't take it personally, it's just how he is."

Derek pushed away from the table and snagged his jacket, shrugging into it quickly. "Go compile that data. I'll catch you Monday," he said as he slung his computer bag over his shoulder.

She followed him out and took the few steps to her office, which happened to be between Derek and Owen's offices. She'd noticed the cars in the parking lot when she arrived at Off the Grid, but she hadn't thought much of it. In the short time she'd been here, she noticed a number of staff worked odd hours. She hadn't considered Owen would be here and mentally chastised herself for not paying atten-tion to which cars were here. With Derek leaving, she thought she might be the only one here with Owen. *Whatever. You're just here to work and that's what you're doing.*

She tossed her jacket onto one of the chairs and sat down at her worktable. She'd quickly come to love the set up in her office. She could easily switch from using her own laptop to using the wide computer screens mounted on her worktable with wireless syncing between the systems. She slipped her shoes off and hooked her feet around the base of her chair. Within minutes, she was completely absorbed in her work.

She'd lost track of time when she heard the whisper of Owen's office door opening. Owen leaned in the doorway to her office. She glanced up and her breath caught. His blue eyes stood out in the dim light, his chiseled features strong in the shadows. Her efforts at taking her mind off of him were blown to bits in less than a second.

He nodded toward her computer screen. "How's that data looking?"

For a moment, she was puzzled. That's how much he threw her off. She temporarily forgot what she'd been working on and why and simply stared at him. One of his dark brows rose, cueing her to the fact she was staring blankly at him. *Wake up Ivy! You look like a fool right about now. Data, he asked about the data.*

"Oh right. Derek sent over everything from the last few batches of data on the test projects. I'd like it to look better. We're still not much above seventy-five percent for pure recycled energy on discharge. I'm convinced we can get it to one hundred, but I need some time to review the designs. That's what I started doing," she said, gesturing to the screen.

Owen pushed off the door and strode into her office. He caught the back of a chair and spun it beside hers. With a few taps on her screen, he pulled up the original designs for the project. Before she knew it, they were in a back and forth about ideas to modify the design. She couldn't quite tamp down the hum Owen set to life in her body and nearly squirmed in her chair to have him sitting right beside her.

She didn't realize how close she'd gotten to him until she felt the brush of his shoulder against hers. He was gesturing at the computer screen and explaining something. 'Something' was about all she could say he was talking about because she completely lost track. He'd barely brushed her arm, and the heat radiating from him nearly singed her. Her pulse rocketed, and her breath hitched. As if he sensed something, he slowly spun in his chair, his knees bumping hers as he did.

Owen's eyes locked with hers, and the air came alive around them. His shoulders rose and fell with a breath, while she could barely catch hers. She could hardly think, but what little grip she had on thought, she tried to tell herself she needed to push her chair back and snap this moment. Yet, she couldn't.

The space around them felt electric. Inside, heat seared through her. His voice broke into the quiet. "I..." He stopped and shook his head sharply. With a muttered imprecation, he grabbed the arms of her chair and gave them a swift tug, pulling her flush against his chair. Before she grasped what was happening, he slid his hand into her hair and fit his mouth over hers. Though more than a week had passed since his first surprise kiss, it was as if they picked up right where they left off. The simmering desire she'd been battling flashed to flame. His tongue swept into her mouth on a gasp, and she was lost—lost in the searing intensity of his kiss, lost in the tidal wave of need he elicited, and nearly overcome with raw longing.

He kissed her as if she were the very air he needed to breathe, his tongue stroking masterfully against hers. By the time he tore his lips away and blazed a scalding trail of kisses along her neck and to the edge of her collar, she was nearly boneless. Her channel clenched, throbbing with need. He lifted his head, his eyes catching hers in a blur of blue. His expression was intent as he stared at her, his eyes searching. As if he'd seen the answer to his unspoken question, he stood swiftly, lifting her into his arms as he did. Being held against the hard planes of his body was a heaven she hadn't imagined.

He took three long strides and sat down in one of the cushioned chairs with her in his lap. He brushed her tangled hair away from her face. Her breath was coming in fitful gasps with heat scoring through her center. His fingers sifted through her hair and traced along the sensitive skin behind her ear, a shiver chasing in the wake of his touch. He traced down along her neck, his fingertip following along her collarbone. His touch was like a ribbon of fire on her skin. He followed along the edge of her shirt, a V-neck fitted skiing top that zipped in the center. By the time he reached the top of the zipper, she was nearly wild with need inside. He hooked his finger over the top of the zipper and dragged it down in slow motion. In a distant corner of her mind, so distant as to be almost inaudible, she heard herself saying she should stop this. But she couldn't. The moment had captured her—she couldn't turn away. It felt so electric and so right.

Cool air rushed against her skin when the zipper fell open. Owen's breath hissed as he pushed her shirt apart. She was typically quite practical when it came to clothes, but she indulged herself when it came to lingerie. She wore a black sheer lace bra. Her nipples were tight and peaked against the silky lace. Owen seemed to be in as much of a trance as she was. He stared for a long moment, his dark blue gaze flicking to hers and back down before he traced a slow circle around a nipple, rolling the other between his thumb and forefinger. A low moan escaped from her, unbidden. As she cast about for something to contain the need galloping through her, he dipped his head and swirled his tongue around her nipple. She cried out and gripped his head in her hands. She was drenched with need and desperate for more. After he spent several heated moments driving her to near madness, teasing her nipples through the lace, he flicked his thumb under the clasp.

She cried out when he drew a nipple into his mouth.

Desire held her fast in its wild grip. She shifted restlessly in his lap, feeling the hard, hot length of him against her hips. With her body moving of its own accord, she spun and straddled him, sighing when she felt the friction of his hard cock against the center of her need. He bit down softly on her nipple and lifted his head, his eyes locking with hers. The air around them was taut, nearly vibrating with the pounding desire between them. She couldn't look away as he dragged his hand down her abdomen and pushed past the waistband of her fitted ski pants. He shoved her panties out of the way and stroked a finger through her folds, which were slick with need.

Another moan escaped as he sank his finger into her channel, followed with a low cry when he stretched her further with a second finger. Everything narrowed to him, to this, to now—while his fingers expertly played her, delving into her channel again and again and again. She was chasing after a pleasure so intense, she couldn't have stopped if she had to.

She hadn't realized her eyes had fallen closed until he said her name. She barely managed to open them, so lost was she in the spiral of pleasure he wrought within her. He circled his thumb over her clit, and that was it. Her channel pulsed and clenched around his fingers, pleasure ripping through her—so sharp it bordered on pain. He slowly stilled as her body relaxed.

Looking into his eyes, she became suddenly aware of what had just happened. She started to wiggle away, but he curled a hand on her hip, holding her in place. "Wait." The low timbre of his voice sent a shiver over her skin. She forced herself to look up again to find him waiting. He slowly slid his hand out of her. She felt the loss of his touch acutely, instantly missing it. He was quiet for several beats. "I didn't mean to let that go so far, but I'm not sorry."

His words startled her. She couldn't say what she'd

expected, but it wasn't that. Seeing as she hadn't ever thought she could be this susceptible to a kiss making her lose her mind with need over a man, it was safe to say she was unprepared. She finally managed to nod.

He watched her, his eyes searching. It felt as if he could see right through her—into the confusion swirling in her thoughts. Rising out of the confusion one feeling rang like a bell—loud and clear. It didn't make sense, it confused her, it worried her, and no matter how many times she tried to think of it any other way, letting herself explore the roaring desire between them felt forbidden. So forbidden it made him even more tempting. She became aware of where she was again—straddling his lap, his cock hot and hard against her. He'd just sent her spinning into a whirl of pleasure, still echoing in soft tremors through her body.

Owen slid his palms down her thighs, his touch warming her. Ivy felt bare and exposed with her shirt hanging open and started to reach to zip it. He beat her to it, carefully pulling her bra back into place and sliding her zipper up. The moment felt so intimate, she didn't know how to react. Her breath became shallow again, and she tried to collect herself. Not the easiest thing to do when she was sitting on his lap, wondering if she had finally found a way to ditch her stupid virginity—a small problem she found incredibly inconvenient. She'd never set out to stay a virgin until she was almost thirty, but life got in the way, or rather, her unyielding focus on academics, research and relentlessly working to get a toehold in the engineering field.

She'd hoped she would finally find time to perhaps explore the dating scene after she finished her graduate degree, yet she'd shut down and tried to hide any glimmer of interest in anyone once things got uncomfortable at the university. After all that, here she was on her new boss's lap wondering if she'd completely lost her mind.

Owen's voice broke into her train of thought. "Just so you know, I don't do things like this. Ever." His tone was somber.

Uncertain how to respond, she said the only thing she could. "Me neither. I don't want you to think I…"

He shook his head sharply. "I don't think anything. Well, except maybe we need to move before I lose control again." His mouth curled in a slow smile, sending her belly in a somersault.

She didn't want to move, she *really* didn't want to move. Yet, she knew he was right. They'd already blown past too many boundaries. Her cheeks were hot as she looked back at him, but she managed to nod and shimmy off his lap quickly. She felt unsteady on her feet, her body still reverberating from the force of her climax. He remained where he was, shifting his hips and straightening his jeans. Uncertain what to do, she crossed her arms and sat down in the chair beside him, tucking her feet under her.

It was oddly comfortable to sit here in the quiet with him. She was definitely unsettled by what had just happened, and her body craved more, but Owen was easy to be around. After a few beats, he spoke again. "I told myself that wouldn't happen again. I'd like to say it won't now, but I'm not so sure about that."

For the first time ever, she saw a hint of uncertainty flash in the back of his eyes. "I know you haven't been here long, but you're a good fit for the team and I want you to stay. I, uh, didn't expect to have…" He paused and gestured between them. "…*this* happen."

Ivy's mind spun, not sure what he was saying. He cleared his throat. "Here's what I think: we just need to let this burn out. It will. If you're worried I'd let something like this interfere with your work, there's no need. It won't."

She stared at him, not sure where he was going with this. "I…um…what do you mean?"

"You set the rules. If you tell me to back the hell off, I will." His mouth hooked at one corner in a wry smile. "But I'll be the first to say, we can burn this out faster the other way."

A laugh bubbled up, startling her. He was offering her the almost perfect way to ditch her virginity. A tiny voice in the far reaches of her mind called out that she was flat crazy if she thought she could do this, but she trusted Owen. She'd already seen how clearly he separated the personal from his work. If they actually let this play out, she'd probably be less distracted at work. Instead of obsessing over him, she could just get him out of her system once and for all. Her laugh faded, and she bit her lip, wondering how honest to be with him. Still buzzing from their encounter and buoyed by a recklessness she rarely indulged, she threw caution to the wind.

With her cheeks flushing and a nervous smile, she caught his eyes. "Okay. Good plan. We'll burn it out and stick to business after that. There's one thing you should know though."

"What's that?"

"I'm a virgin."

CHAPTER 7

Owen stood in front of the windows in his office, staring through the gap in the trees where a slice of Kachemak Bay was visible. The sky was dappled with clouds with the sun striking sparks on the surface of the water. Usually the view settled him. He loved the peace offered by the spectacular natural beauty here. Aside from skiing, he'd been drawn to Alaska because its wildness and beauty offered him an easy escape mentally. Today, nothing helped. He was restless, unfocused and still stunned at Ivy's admission last night.

She was a virgin, and he was damned straight to hell because that huge detail only made him want her so badly he was close to physical pain. The fact that her honesty hadn't sent him running only flummoxed him further. His preference for keeping relationships entirely casual didn't include getting involved with a virgin. Before that startling detail, he'd shocked himself with the mental gymnastics he did to come up with the idea that he could find a way to get Ivy out of his system. Nearly drowning in the wave of raw need Ivy elicited, he'd needed something to latch onto. She'd pleasantly surprised him by quickly agreeing. He didn't sense she was inclined toward anything more than he was. They'd get this rampaging out-of-control lust out of the way and move on.

Then, Ivy went and told him she was a virgin, and he didn't know what the hell to do now. It should've thrown ice water on his desire. Really, virginity was something he didn't want to handle—it made things feel way too personal. She dismissed it as if it was an inconvenient problem she hadn't found time to deal with. He'd barely slept last night, tossing and turning, his mind running on its own private treadmill. He'd yet to come to a conclusion. Part of him screamed out he was crazy to even consider his off the cuff idea to get Ivy out of his system. That part thought he was even more insane now that he knew she was a virgin. So there was that and the fact he wanted her with a ferocity that ran so deep he couldn't turn away.

At the sound of a knock at his door, he spun away from the windows. Joan gave a small wave through the glass. He gestured for her to come in and strode to lean against his worktable. Joan stepped through the door and closed it quietly behind her. She walked to stand in front of him. Her warm brown gaze scanned him, a hint of concern there. She tapped her foot lightly on the floor before finally speaking. "Okay, what's wrong?"

If it had been anyone other than Joan, Owen would have ignored the question. It wasn't likely anyone other than Joan would even ask, except maybe Derek. But Joan was Joan, one of the few people he didn't keep at arms length. Joan wouldn't let him even if he tried, but he didn't. She and Reggie had helped him get through the darkest, most lonely time of his life and he'd never forget it.

He met Joan's eyes with a sigh. "I dunno. Just trying to figure some things out."

"What things?"

He shrugged, and Joan's eyes narrowed. "It's Ivy, isn't it?"

He should've been surprised, but he wasn't. Joan was practically a mind reader. Most of the time, it amused him, but right now, it annoyed him.

"What makes you think it has anything to do with Ivy?"

"Well, if I wasn't sure before, I am now."

Owen forced himself to take a slow breath, trying to keep from losing his cool. "Why do you say that?"

Joan crossed her arms and glared at him. "When you're avoiding, you answer questions with questions. Fine. Maybe you don't want to talk about it, but you don't have to be an asshole to everyone around the office. It's been two days and you're like a cactus—if anyone gets too close, they get pricked. You're not asking what I think, but I'll tell you. There's some serious chemistry between you two. You hide it well, but it's there and you don't know what the hell to do about it. If you ask me, it's about damn time someone got through those walls you put up. If there was ever a woman perfect for you, it's Ivy. She's brilliant, she's just as passionate about her work as you are, and she's a sweetheart."

Owen pushed away from his desk and started pacing back and forth. Hearing Joan say Ivy was perfect for him made him want to bolt from the room. At the same time, he couldn't have argued against Ivy's brilliance and passion and that soft side he saw every so often. He almost wanted to kick his heart out of his body at how much he longed to stop fighting against the yearning he felt for her. Joan leaned against his worktable and stayed quiet while he paced for a few moments. He finally stopped and rolled his head from side to side in an effort to ease the tension bundled in his neck and shoulders. "Fine. I might be a bit rattled about Ivy. If you don't mind, I'd rather not talk about it. It's bad enough you got me to admit it."

Joan's eyes softened as she nodded slowly. "Fair enough.

Take it easy on yourself, okay." After that, Joan quickly moved on. She knew him well enough to know he didn't like dwelling on anything personal. "Well then, try being a little nicer around here, okay? Derek's tied up on a conference call, and he asked me to grab some coffee. I came to see if you wanted some."

"Of course."

She pushed her hips away from the table and stood. "I'll grab the usual from Misty Mountain Café. Need anything else?"

"How about you pick up some lunch for everyone?"

"You got it." Joan started to turn away and spun back. Stepping to Owen's side, she gave him a quick hug. Leaning back, she squeezed his shoulders before stepping away. "Nice to know there's a chink in your armor." At that, she turned on her heel and walked away, her cowboy boots echoing on the tiled floor.

The door clicked shut behind her, and Owen leaned his head back with a sigh. He needed to focus on something other than obsessing about Ivy. He shook his head in wonderment. Concentration wasn't something he struggled with, not when it came to work. He squared his shoulders and took a deep breath. Much as he didn't want to deal with anyone else right now, the best way to get his mind back on track was to throw himself into a project. He strode out of his office and down the hallway. He was relieved to see Ivy wasn't in her office, otherwise the pull to walk in there would be overwhelming. As it was, his eyes flicked through the doorway, honing in on the chair where she'd straddled him and he'd felt almost drugged by the slick heat of her. With a sharp shake of his head, he looked away and aimed for the conference room.

He found Derek rolling his eyes at the phone in the center of the table. Owen arched a brow, and Derek leaned forward to tap the mute button, affording them the opportunity to talk while the call droned on. "What's up?" Derek asked as he tossed a ball back and forth between his hands.

Owen sat down beside him and powered up the large screen mounted on the wall at the head of the table. He slid out the keyboard tray under the table and tapped a few keys. Derek unmuted the phone and quickly replied to a comment on the call before muting the speakers again. He glanced up at the screen. "Aha. You wanna work on those now?" he asked with a grin.

The 'those' Derek was referring to were Owen's latest plans for a new wind collection system. He and Derek had been tinkering with these for the last few months with the goal to design a form of wind turbine that was small enough to hang on a tree, almost like an ornament. In moments, he and Derek were deep into a discussion, interspersed in between Derek's contributions to the conference call. Owen finally managed to knock his mind off the loop of Ivy.

Joan poked her head in to drop off their coffees and slide a pizza box on the table. Hours later, Owen leaned back in his chair and stretched his arms overhead. Derek had left a few minutes prior, and he was relieved to have finally had a few hours where his mind behaved like it should. He decided not to tempt fate and leave before he found himself pacing in his office again.

* * *

IVY CARRIED two glasses of wine to the couch in Ginger and Cam's house, handing one to Ginger and the other to Marley Hamilton. Marley was Ginger's best friend and married to Gage who ran the ski lodge where Cam worked. It was a snowy evening, and Marley had stopped by for visit. As Ivy turned to go back to the kitchen, a small pair of arms encircled her legs, almost sending her to the floor.

"Well, hey Holly," she said as she glanced down to find Marley's daughter grinning up at her.

Holly grinned and gurgled something. Holly bore a strong resemblance to her mother with the same auburn hair and lively green eyes. Ivy leaned over and lifted Holly into her arms. "Oh my, you are getting big!"

Holly gurgled again and promptly latched onto a chunk of Ivy's hair as if it was there solely for her to hang onto. Ivy heard Marley's laugh as she returned to the kitchen. Ivy snagged her own glass of wine and made her way back into the living room, sitting down in the corner of the sectional with Holly in her lap. Holly promptly crawled off and made a beeline for her mother who was sitting between Ivy and Ginger.

Marley handed Holly a stuffed frog, which Holly promptly grabbed onto. Marley glanced over at Ivy. "She's getting pretty heavy, huh?"

Ivy grinned. "Sure is."

Marley shook her head softly. "I can't believe she's over a year now."

Ginger eyed Marley and Holly. "Even though I see her a few times a week, she's bigger every time." She paused for a sip of wine and switched topics. "Did you say Gage was going to Anchorage soon?"

"He plans a run up there for a few days next week. Need anything?" Marley asked in return.

Ginger leaned over and pulled a notepad and pen off the coffee table. "Sure do! Let me get you a list right now."

Ivy glanced between them. "What's the big deal with shopping in Anchorage?"

Ginger grinned. "Have you paid attention to the prices around here? It's obscene. Anchorage is the closest place to get halfway normal prices on stuff. Our pantry's getting bare, so we need to stock up."

"Oh, is that why you have such a big pantry?" Ivy asked.

She'd thought it wonderful, but the walk-in pantry in Ginger's kitchen was definitely larger than normal, not to mention there were two chest freezers in the garage.

"Exactly," Ginger replied as she quickly jotted down a long list.

Marley glanced to Ivy. "Do you need anything? Gage'll be happy to make a few extra stops."

Ivy laughed and shook her head. "Nope. Seeing as I'm mooching off Ginger and Cam, I'm all set. Maybe before next winter when I try to find my own place, but until then I'm good."

Conversation moved on with occasional distractions offered by Holly as she made her way from the couch to the floor and giggled while George bounced around her in a circle. Ivy was relieved for the distraction of Marley's visit. She needed something to get her mind off of Owen and not much did. In the month or so she'd been in Diamond Creek, she'd discovered Ginger and Cam had a relaxed, but somewhat busy social world. Friends often stopped by the house, and Ginger had already insisted Ivy accompany them to several dinners up at the ski lodge. The longer Ivy was here, the more she liked it. She'd always had a close circle of friends, yet the deeper she got into her graduate studies, the harder it was to find time for a social life. The few friends she had came from her narrow work life before. The climb up the academic ladder was slow and grueling, so she'd known she was in for the long haul when she accepted the faculty position.

Her work life at Off the Grid was markedly different than what she'd been accustomed to. Instead of hours buried in research assigned by others and tolerating menial assignments, she was given free rein to work on projects. Owen's leadership at the firm was clear. He set the priorities for projects and assigned team leaders and moved on. Beyond the work on the battery projects, she'd come to understand she could do her own exploratory research in other areas as long as it had something to do with sustainable energy.

Gone were the days of worrying about faculty meetings where senior faculty droned on, the days of following antiquated protocols and making sure she didn't ruffle the feathers of senior faculty even if the faculty in question were verging on senility. The best of all, she was free from Dr. Parkhursts's leering perusal of her and his occasional advances. She'd almost forgotten about the formal harassment complaint she'd filed until she received a call from the Human Resources Department with an update on the status —a most pointless update since nothing had changed. They were still 'investigating.' Ivy experienced a flash of bitterness, wondering if they actually were even bothering to investigate anything.

With a mental shake, she tried to bring herself back to the moment, half-listening while Marley talked about a coding project she was working on. Thinking about work was a tad too appealing though, so Ivy's thoughts skipped from how much she loved her new job to her angst over what to do about this thing between her and Owen. She didn't know what to call it other than a thing. She was now convinced she'd gone completely crazy by telling Owen she was a virgin. The giddy moment where she persuaded herself it was a good idea to just get him out of her system had deflated swiftly once she saw the look in his eyes. He'd looked completely shocked. He'd managed to be polite and even somehow made it seem not so awkward. But he'd barely looked at her in the days since.

She was trying to come around to the fact that it was probably all for the best. She was mortified now—what with all but melting in his lap the other night and then being stupid enough to tell him the truth. It was embarrassing enough that she was actually a virgin, even worse it was only because she truly hadn't found the time to have a relationship. She'd have felt better if it had been because she was trying to keep it that way. But no. It was all because she was busy, that and the fact that most men's eyes glazed over once she started talking about her work. Of course, Owen was the opposite. The moment she started talking about projects and data, his focus was so absolute, it thrilled her beyond belief. On the heels of another mental sigh, she forced herself to stop thinking about Owen and listen to Marley and Ginger.

"...so if I can tweak the code to be more responsive to sounds, I think it might be what you're after," Marley finished.

"What are you working on?" Ivy asked. She knew from Ginger that Marley was a computer whiz and did freelance coding and website building for work.

Ginger glanced over as she set her wineglass down and pulled her hair up into a knot on top of her head. She caught Ivy's eyes with a sly grin. "You were totally zoned out! We've only been talking about this for more than five minutes. Let me guess, daydreaming about Owen again?"

Ivy couldn't have stopped the blush from heating her cheeks if she tried. She rolled her eyes and took a gulp of wine. "I was enjoying the view and not really paying attention. That's all."

Ginger cocked her head to the side and looked as if she was about to keep teasing, but she must've taken pity on Ivy because she let the topic of Owen drop. "I asked Marley to see if she could come up with an app for speech therapy. Because she's awesome, she's been working on it in her free time. If it works out, I'll be able to set it up for parents to help them work on speech exercises at home with kids."

"Oh, that's so cool!" Ivy exclaimed, swinging her gaze to Marley. "Ginger mentioned you do coding for apps and stuff. What other types of projects do you do?"

Marley quickly launched into a summary, lifting a sleepy Holly into her lap as she did. Conversation moved onto Marley asking about Ivy's adjustment to Off the Grid. "I've heard it's a great place to work, but aside from Joan, I haven't really gotten to know anyone there. Owen skis a lot and his friend Derek comes along sometimes. Joan told me she didn't even think twice when Owen announced plans to move the firm to Alaska. I figured it might've been a big change for her since they used to be in Boston, but she said she always wanted to try living outside of the city and they love it here. Owen certainly keeps to himself though. Gage mentioned he only came into the lodge restaurant for the first time last weekend. What's this about Owen anyway?" Marley's eyes held a soft gleam. She wasn't quite as bold as Ginger when it came to teasing, but she didn't shy away from it.

Ivy leaned back into the cushions and sighed. "What did Ginger tell you?" she asked with an accusatory glare at Ginger.

Marley laughed softly and shook her head. "Nothing, except for what she just said a few minutes ago. Owen's managed the impossible. He's handsome, he moved here from out of state and he appears to be loaded. But he's kept such a low profile, the gossip's not too bad. So…?"

Ivy shook her head and fought to keep from blushing. It was bad enough when Ginger picked up on her interest in him, but that was before she'd been half-naked in front of him. She finally shrugged. "Nothing I can do anything about anyway."

Ginger cocked her head to the side. "I thought we straightened that out. You're a contract employee. It's not like he's technically your superior."

Ivy rolled her eyes again. "You're being silly. It's a technicality. It doesn't change the fact I don't want to mess up the best job I've ever had. I don't need things to get weird because I happen to think Owen's handsome."

Marley jumped in. "Well, Delia said Owen could hardly stop staring at you last weekend at the lodge, so it doesn't sound like this is a one-way thing."

Ivy closed her eyes and leaned her head back against the couch. When she opened them, she followed the pattern of knots in the pine ceiling before lifting her head again. "It still doesn't matter. Am I going to have to worry about gossip like this all the time? I can't believe Delia noticed anything. She was busy running back and forth the whole time we were there."

Ginger snorted. "You can't live in Diamond Creek and be new around town without people getting curious. It'll pass. But don't worry about Delia. She might say something to Marley or me, but otherwise she'll keep quiet."

"I wasn't worried about her, it's just weird anyone would notice."

Ginger shrugged. "I did. That man could win an award for smoldering. He was subtle, but damn, he nearly undressed you with his eyes. I was there too, you know."

Ivy's face was on fire and her belly somersaulted just thinking about what came to pass after their impromptu lunch at the ski lodge. She shook her head and grabbed her almost empty wineglass from the coffee table to finish it off. "It doesn't matter because it's not going anywhere," she said firmly. "It'll pass because it has to. In my whole life, I've never even noticed someone I worked with like that. Even worse, after what happened with Dr. Parkhurst, I can't even think about this."

"Dr. Parkhurst is an ancient asshole who gets his kicks fantasizing about women young enough to be his daughter. Since he was officially your boss, he had all kinds of power to make your life miserable if you didn't give him what he wanted.

I get your whole thing about not wanting to make things messy with Owen, but don't even think about comparing the two. They're not even close to the same thing," Ginger said emphatically. "Anyway, what *is* going on with the complaint you filed? You haven't said anything about it recently."

Ivy sighed and slumped into the couch, curling her feet underneath her. "The HR people called me with what they said was an update, but the update is they're still investigating. Sometimes I wonder if I should've bothered with filing a formal complaint. It's not like I ever want to go back there."

"I'm glad you did," Marley said firmly. "I didn't spend as much time as you did in the university world, but I saw how ugly it could get in grad school. Some professors were so blatant, it was disgusting. The only way it will change is if people are held accountable. I'm sure it sucks, but in the end it's a good thing. Lucky for you, you landed on your feet."

"I know. All in all, it ended up being a good thing that I left." Ivy swung to Ginger. "Which is why I don't want to mess up the good thing I have here."

Ginger laughed and stood to get another bottle of wine from the kitchen. Marley demurred, declaring she needed to head home before the roads got too bad.

Later that night, Ivy sat propped up on the pillows in her bed in the guest bedroom. Ginger and Cam had gone to bed a while ago with George bounding up the stairs behind them. Ivy was restless, so she curled up with her laptop and tried to work. Wind was blowing mightily outside, pelting icy snow against the windows. It was hard to believe spring was technically right around the corner. Having grown up in the mountains of Utah, Ivy was accustomed to late winter snowstorms such as this one, although she was surprised at its force. The coastal winds were brutal here in the winter. She tugged the blanket closer and pulled up another set of data. Off the Grid had set up test projects in various locations around the world. Between Owen and Derek's connections from United Tech, they knew engineers everywhere, most of whom were happy to help with testing new designs. Ivy loved that she could pull up remote data and analyze results whenever she wanted.

As she pored over and compared results from a few different designs, she noticed someone else was working in the reports as well. With her remote log in, she was able to log onto Off the Grid's private network from home, so it was as if she was there. Curious to see who else might be working close to midnight, she clicked the icon that would tell her. Her pulse lunged and heat slid through her veins when she saw Owen's name. *Really? You're that ridiculous? It's midnight and you're getting hot and bothered all because he happens to be logged on at the same time as you. You seriously need to move on. It's obvious he's not interested.* On the heels of her well-trained, definitely not reckless side having its say, her newly emboldened, definitely reckless side offered its own thoughts. *Why do I need to move on? Maybe it's not so crazy to try to get him out of my system. I might as well have fun if I'm going to finally find time to ditch my stupid virginity. And I know it will be fun if it's Owen.*

Just thinking that thought sent a flash of heat through her, and liquid need clenching within her channel. Dear God. It was bad. She was sitting here all by herself and nearly desperate for release when moments ago she'd been thinking about batteries and output. Her finger hovered over the icon where she could click and instant message him. Before she even considered what she was doing, she tapped it and quickly typed a greeting.

Hey, what are you doing working so late?

His reply was swift.

I could ask the same of you. Compared the test results yet?

In the middle of it. The results from the test product in Barrow look the most promising.

Noticed the same thing. That's the only one we have out from the modifications you first suggested.

Ivy hadn't known that. She was still getting her footing at work and wasn't accustomed to how quickly projects in test phases could move. A flush of pride rose within her.

Really? Wow, that was fast.

Really. You think fast. We work fast.

Ivy could practically feel his smile. He was miles away, either at the office or at home, and they had nothing more than the ephemeral link of a computer connection, yet she could *feel* him.

Her breath became short with her pulse running away from her. She unconsciously clenched her thighs together, trying to quell the need there. That only made things worse because she remembered the feel of Owen's fingers teasing her to an explosive climax.

Not thinking, what she typed next startled her, and she wanted to take it back as soon as she hit enter to send the message.

I hope things are okay. Didn't mean to weird you out the other night.

The first pause in their back and forth occurred. It couldn't have been that long, but she berated herself the entire time. What the hell was she thinking? It would've been much better if she just ignored what happened and let it fade away. She almost closed her laptop, thinking maybe she could simply pretend she'd never said anything, when she saw the symbol that indicated he was typing a reply.

Not weird. Sorry if it seemed like it. We should talk. Dinner tomorrow?

Ivy must've re-read his reply about fifty times inside of a few minutes as she stared at her computer screen. With her definitely reckless side firmly in control, she didn't even stop to think once she gathered herself enough to respond.

Sure. Where?

My place. I'll cook.

Don't know where you live.

Keep driving past Off the Grid, take the first driveway on the left.

Okay. What time?

6. Back to my point. You do great work. Signing off now.

Ivy watched as his name switched to inactive, staring for far too long at the window that contained their conversation. Inside, flutters were spinning in her belly, her heart was pounding and heat streaked through her.

CHAPTER 8

$\mathcal{O}$wen ran a hand through his hair and leaned back, spinning in a slow circle in his chair. "I dunno. You think we can have this ready by next week?" he asked, spinning to face Derek who sat across from him at the conference table. It was Saturday afternoon and he'd been in the office all day. Derek had stopped in for a bit, and they were considering sending the latest design for their wind turbine project to the assembly team.

Derek shrugged. "Maybe, maybe not. I say let's get started."

"Okay. Let's do it."

Owen angled to face the computer screen and tapped a few keys to send the files off. "Perfect. Glad you stopped by today."

Derek pushed his chair back and stood. "Good timing." He leaned against the doorframe and eyed Owen. "Ivy's fitting in great. The team loves her. Before you brought her on, I admit I was a little worried. After what we went through with John..." He trailed off and shrugged.

Derek was referring to the last engineer they'd tried to

add to the team. John came with amazing references. Once he started at Off the Grid, it became immediately clear being a part of a team was of zero interest to John. Owen had moved quickly to terminate his contract, but John fought over the negotiations. His arrogance was damaging to the rest of the team, and he challenged Owen at every turn. They'd been so burned by the experience, Owen hadn't even tried to recruit again for over a year. He'd finally given in when it became obvious the engineering team didn't have enough support to function as it should. Outside of Joan, Derek was the only person at Off the Grid Owen consulted with about new hires. He relied on Joan for feedback about the entire staff, while he turned to Derek for feedback about engineers. Derek had made a few calls about Ivy, coming up with nothing other than glowing references. Even though they still had reservations, they'd gone ahead.

Owen met Derek's eyes and nodded. "I've heard the same. Damn relieved she's working out."

Derek straightened again. "I see you're still playing it cool."

Owen bit back a sigh and shook his head. "Leave it alone."

Derek grinned. "It's nice to see you're human." He didn't give Owen a chance to respond and called over his shoulder as he walked out of Owen's office. "Catch ya later."

Owen watched Derek leave and stood from his chair, walking to stand in front of the windows. It wasn't unusual for him to work a lot, in fact it was more typical than not. Yet, he'd been working almost relentlessly since his kiss and then some with Ivy earlier in the week. Even by his standards, it was a bit much. Then, she'd messaged him late last night, or early this morning, depending on how you wanted to look at it. He'd been at the end of his rope as far as getting a handle on his near obsession with her and impulsively decided to invite her for dinner. He'd tipped over into the decision he'd been on the verge of all week. It was clear there was no getting Ivy out of his system unless he acted. If anything, the burning desire she elicited was only getting worse.

He also had this weird, completely foreign protectiveness about her. Every time he thought about someone else sharing her first time with her, he nearly lost his mind. Not that he thought he deserved it, but he couldn't stand to let someone have what he wanted.

He stared blindly out over the view. The jagged peaks across the bay loomed in the cloudy sky. He glanced at his watch. He needed to get to the store and get home in time to start dinner. Though he rarely shared dinner with others, he enjoyed cooking. His mother had loved to cook, and he'd spent many childhood hours with her in the kitchen. His chest felt tight for a moment, the warm memory of his mother and those hours with her sending a pang of sadness through him.

He shifted his shoulders and rolled his head side to side before taking a deep breath and turning to stride out of his office. Roughly an hour later, he was in the middle of sautéing vegetables when the doorbell chimed. He turned the flame on the burner down and wiped his hands quickly before walking to the door.

He swung it open. Ivy stood there, her amber hair falling in loose waves around her shoulders. She so often had it tied back that every time he saw it loose, he had to fight not to run his hands through the silky locks. She lifted her head and smiled, a hint of uncertainty flashing in the depths of her eyes.

IVY LOOKED UP AT OWEN, his jet back hair gleaming under the light from inside and his bright blue eyes catching hers and sending a jolt of heat through her center. She smiled, warmth blossoming when the corner of his mouth hitched up. He was so often somber, any smile felt like a surprise gift. "Come on in," he said, turning to the side and gesturing her in.

She looked around as she followed him inside. From the outside, his home was gorgeous—a three-story circular house with light gray siding. It was tucked into the hillside above Diamond Creek, built partially into the hill, which she would bet had been the plan as a way to use the natural protection of the earth to minimize energy consumption. The entry to the home was on the middle floor. She glanced around, noticing the entire floor was mostly open with only one door to the side of the kitchen. A massive soapstone fireplace anchored the center of the area with an open kitchen to one side, a dining room table roughly in the center on the back, and couches and chairs with tables scattered amongst them to the other side of the fireplace. The space was open and inviting with a modern feel.

She followed Owen toward the kitchen area, which had a counter against the wall and an island with stools where the stove was. It was obvious he was already cooking some-thing. She didn't know why but it surprised her he'd offered to cook. He was clearly comfortable in the kitchen as he spun a spice rack and added some to the vegetables he was sautéing. He gestured for her to have a seat across from where he was stationed.

"What are you making?" she asked as she slipped her coat off and hung it on the back of the stool before sitting down. She rested her elbows on the counter and watched as he added yet another spice to whatever he was making.

"I realized I probably should've asked what you wanted for dinner. Since I didn't, I went with something simple. Veggie and chicken stir-fry. I know you're not a vegetarian because you had some of the buffalo chicken pizza at lunch last week, so I figured this would be safe."

"It smells amazing. Do you cook much?"

He shrugged, those muscled shoulders of his rising and falling. She couldn't help but stare. She rarely had a chance to look at him because, well, it wouldn't do for her to stare when they were at work together. At the moment, he was occupied looking at what he was doing, so she had more free rein than normal. He wore a bright blue long-sleeved t-shirt, which just happened to bring out his eyes. Not as if they needed help being brought out. Ridiculous as it was, a simple t-shirt emphasized his cut body. She figured he must work out because hours in front of a computer didn't give him the sculpted body he had. Her belly tightened just looking at him, and she tore her eyes away.

"Not as much as I'd like, actually. As you know, I work a lot. Doesn't leave much time for cooking. When I get the chance, I do." The low timbre of his voice sent a prickle over her skin.

"Not to ask the obvious, but where'd you learn to cook? Not many guys spend much time on cooking."

His eyes flicked up to meet hers, a flash of pain in their depths that disappeared as quickly as it came. "My mom taught me. She loved to cook, so that's what we did together a lot."

Ivy's heart squeezed, and she felt her own twinge of pain for his loss. She was relieved Derek had shared the story of Owen's parents, or she might have stumbled here. What she didn't know was how to navigate whether Owen knew what she knew. While she was considering what to say, he filled in the blank for her.

"My parents died when I was in college. Cooking is one of my best memories of my mom."

His openness surprised her. "I'm so sorry. That must've been difficult."

That flash of pain came and went again in his gaze when he nodded. "It was. You get used to it eventually though."

"You do. My older brother died a few years ago. It was really hard on our family."

His eyes flicked up again, this time holding hers. For a long moment, he simply stared at her and then nodded. "I'm sorry about your brother. Cam mentioned him to me."

After another beat, he turned off the burner and looked away. Ivy didn't want to dwell on a painful topic, so she waited to see what he might say next. As he added chicken he must've cooked before her arrival to the vegetables, he moved on to talking about the data from the modified design on the battery project.

A while later, she leaned over to look at the computer tablet Owen was holding. They'd had dinner, which was absolutely delicious. They'd relocated into the living room and were seated on the couch, which she discovered was ridiculously comfortable with its luxurious pillows. She'd had a few glasses of wine and managed to relax. They still hadn't talked about anything to do with them. Unfortunately, she was awash in the bubble of desire that hovered around them whenever they happened to be alone. She'd like to think focusing on research with him would get her mind off of the raw longing he elicited, but it was so rare to find a man with the same level of passion she felt for her research *and* be physically attractive to her, it only made it worse.

As it was, she was sitting beside him, her breathing shallow and her pulse skittering wildly while he tapped a few icons on the screen and asked her what she thought about the possible output. She could feel the heat of him beside her, and she had to force her mind to focus. He'd just asked her a question and all she'd heard was the low rumble of his sexy voice. She'd never considered anyone's voice sexy and never even thought of the possibility. Owen's was somehow gruff and warm at once, sending hot shivers over her skin.

He cleared his throat. "Ivy?"

She whipped her head up from where she'd been blankly staring at the tablet screen. "Huh?"

"You with me here?" The dark slash of a brow arched up.

"Oh, right. Sorry, got a little distracted," she managed to reply with only a slight hitch in her breathing.

He slowly lowered the computer tablet and set it on the coffee table in front of them. "Maybe we should talk."

Anxiety raced through her, butterflies twirling in her belly. "About what?"

That brow arched again, and he crossed his feet, which were propped on the coffee table. "About us."

"Oh." She bit her lip and tried to casually take a breath. She was short on air and nearly lightheaded as a result.

"Since it doesn't seem like this..." With a pause, he gestured between them. "...thing with us is going away, I think maybe we should do what we said and get it out of our systems."

She was nearly frozen in place, but she somehow managed to nod. Her mind was racing in fits and starts, spinning over the implication of what he'd said.

He searched her face, his eyes dipping down and back up again, her nipples tightening at the feel of his heated gaze. "Just to make it clear, you didn't weird me out the other night. I just wasn't expecting you to announce you were a virgin. No good reason, other than you surprised me. It sounds like you're pretty practical about the whole thing. If you weren't, I'd say trying to get this out of our systems would be a really bad plan. Did I understand you right?"

She swallowed, her heart beating like a bird fluttering wildly in its cage. "Right. It's an inconvenient detail. Between my graduate program, my doctoral program and my brother dying, well, there hasn't been much time for me to think about dating. I just didn't want to go into this thing without you knowing that."

She shocked herself yet again by being so blunt with him.

He nodded, his eyes still locked to hers. He really needed to stop that because it made her body go crazy. Heat suffused her and she could feel the moisture building between her thighs.

"Right then," he finally said. "In that case…"

He moved swiftly, pulling her into his lap where her knees fell to either side. They were right back where they'd been that night in her office. She could feel the hard, hot ridge of him against her core, and she felt a sense of relief to know he was as affected by her as she was him.

CHAPTER 9

Owen was at the end of his restraint. His hold on control had vacillated all evening. Some moments he managed to distract himself, but they were fleeting. He felt her hips settle down against him and could feel the moist heat of her through her leggings. She wore a loose flowing white blouse over leggings and boots, which she'd kicked off by the door. Her blouse should have concealed her curves, but not for him. His eyes kept falling to the shadowed valley between her breasts. Just now, having her this close, he latched onto his restraint. He was finally going to give into what he wanted. Yet, he wouldn't let himself lose control because that would be too much right now. With a gulp of air, he sifted a hand through her hair, the silky threads sliding through his fingers. He scanned her face, his eyes catching on her full lips before he finally dipped his head and kissed her.

Each kiss with her only hammered home the reality he barely had control when it came to Ivy. Kissing her was like a drug. He devoured her mouth, sweeping his tongue inside and glorying in her response. She kissed with wild abandon, her tongue stroking against his and soft moans coming from her throat. Lust tightened like a coil within him. She flexed closer to him when he dragged his hand out of her hair and slid it down her back to curl over her bottom—all lush softness. When she arched against him, her hips rolling over his cock, he growled into her mouth before tearing his lips free. A heated look in her eyes—warm amber flashing with fire—and he tore at her shirt, swearing when one of the buttons caught.

Ivy leaned back and shook her shoulders, her blouse falling down her arms. She wore another ridiculously feminine bra—this one sheer cream lace. Her nipples were taut and pink, easily visible through the flimsy excuse for fabric. He didn't wait and leaned forward to swirl his tongue over the lace, drenching it as he drew the hard nub in his mouth, smiling against her skin when she gripped his hair and moaned. He turned his attention to her other nipple until the lace was damp. Leaning back, he gave himself a moment to savor the rapid rise and fall of her breath with her nipples outlined under the drenched fabric. He could only wait so long before he flicked his thumb under the clasp and her breasts tumbled free. Catching her lips in another kiss, he cupped his hands around her breasts, the skin so soft he groaned into her mouth.

In a blur of need with the whip of lust lashing at him, Owen poured himself into the moment—scalding hot kisses, Ivy arching and flexing in his arms, the blistering need clawing at him—as they yanked and tugged at each other's clothes. Somewhere along the way, he paused and leaned back. She was almost bare, save a pair of panties that matched her bra. Her skin was so silky, glinted with gold in the flickering firelight. Her hair was a tangled mess on the cushions behind her, and he wanted her with a ferocity he'd never experienced. He'd had this idea that once he could let his desire room free, it would ease. Yet, he was finding the opposite, the more he got to taste and experience her, the higher and hotter his need burned.

"Ivy."

Her eyes opened and amber fire looked back at him. With his eyes on her, he hooked a finger over the edge of her panties and slowly dragged them down. She kicked them loose and they joined the clothes scattered on the floor. He stroked a finger through her folds, almost groaning at how wet she was. He'd done a bit of thinking about this whole virginity thing and determined the only way he'd get through this without backing out was to focus entirely on making sure her pleasure was paramount. That was usually his focus when it came to sex, yet he kept things so casual with women, it was more of a goal to make sure no woman walked away unsatisfied. With Ivy, it was that he was determined to make sure she found nothing but pure pleasure.

Her eyes fell closed on a low moan as he slowly eased a finger into her channel. When her hips arched into his touch, he slid another finger inside. With one hand gripping the soft curve of her hip and the other plunging into her channel, he brought his mouth to her. He was lost—lost in the sound of her rough cries, the roll of her hips against his mouth and the clench of her channel around his fingers. She tasted salty and sweet, and he'd barely had enough when she cried out, her body stiffening and her channel tightening around his fingers. She slowly relaxed, and he eased back. Keeping an iron grip on his control—and damn was it hard when he looked at her and saw her gaze hazy with passion and the firelight flickering on her dewy skin— he snagged the condom he'd tucked into his pocket hours ago. Back when he was still wondering if he'd be insane enough to go through with this, back when he'd conveniently forgotten how wildly tempting she was. When they were together and there was nothing other than his own discipline to hold him back, well, that's when he discovered how weak he was.

He stood, regretting the brief moment he wasn't touching her, kicked his briefs off, and rolled the condom on in record time. When he stretched out over her, she opened her eyes again, and he couldn't look away. Her skin was damp with the sheen of her passion, as was his. His heart was pounding so hard, he was surprised he didn't crack a rib. In this moment, he felt spun tight inside a shimmering connection. He'd never experienced a flicker of doubt in a moment such as this. Then, he'd never been with a virgin, Yet, he knew that wasn't what this was. It was Ivy and this nearly overpowering link between them. He eased his weight against her, hanging onto his control when he felt her slick heat. Much as he wanted to surge inside right now, he needed to move slowly. He closed his eyes for a moment, savoring the feel of her luscious body. When he opened them, he reached up and brushed her tangled hair out of her eyes.

"You sure about this?" he asked. He needed to make sure she wasn't having second thoughts. They'd already blown through so many barriers he normally kept firmly in place, he didn't know how they'd roll back to where they'd been before. Yet, he wasn't about to blow through this last one without confirming she was certain.

She bit her lip—lashing the whip of lust within him—and nodded. The head of his cock rested at her entrance already, and he could feel the pulse of her channel. He eased inside just barely. She curled her legs around his hips, inviting him in further. He moved another fraction. She was tight, so damned tight. With his body screaming for more, he held on and forced himself to be still. She flexed against him. He could feel the tension running through her. "You okay?" he managed to ask, his voice rough.

He felt her nod. She shocked him by arching swiftly and

spurring him with her heels. His body reacted reflexively and he surged into her, seating himself fully. He felt her go taut under him, and he started to pull back, but she gripped him tighter. "No! Just stay there."

Owen wasn't much for following instructions, but right now, he did precisely as she requested and held completely still. His heart was still banging away, and he could feel hers against his skin. The moment was so intimate, he was too stunned to consider the implications. He felt her channel slowly ease around him. Only when her legs loosened and her palm slid down his back did he get up the nerve to meet her eyes again.

Her gaze was almost contemplative. She was quiet and lifted a hand to trace one of his brows. As her fingertip traced along his cheekbone, she leaned up and caught his lips in a kiss. They eased into motion. He moved slowly, rocking into her creamy clench. He was still trying to hold onto some restraint, but it was about the most difficult thing he'd ever done. Her soft pants and moans came in between his own broken breathing and rough groans. Her channel clenched around him, tremors rolling through her body. He reached between them and dragged his thumb across her clit. A sharp cry broke and her channel throbbed around him. He unraveled and finally let go, surging deeply within her once more as his release rolled through him in a crashing wave.

* * *

IVY DRIFTED DOWN from the head-spinning, body-melting moments that had just passed. Owen eased away from her, the air cool against her skin when he stepped away. She managed to open her eyes to see him toss his condom in the trashcan by the kitchen counter before striding quickly back to the couch, snagging a fleece throw on the way. He paused by the couch and looked down at her, his blue eyes bright in the dim light. He appeared to be considering something. He nodded, as if to himself, and leaned over, draping the blanket around her and lifting her into his arms.

Her body was still reverberating from what had just happened—the most intense experience of her life. She'd been so casual about getting rid of her inconvenient virginity. She'd treated it as if it was like learning to drive, or something along those lines. She hadn't expected this—this incandescent experience. Even now, it felt as if they were in a shimmering web together. The fleece blanket was soft against her skin, and his body was hard. His muscles flexed as he walked across the room.

"Where are we going?" she finally thought to ask.

He glanced down, and her breath caught. Just that—a passing glance at his chiseled features and need flashed inside again, rising out of the embers of her last climax.

"To bed," he said simply.

"What about the fire?" she asked. She had no idea why her mind went there, but when she was off kilter, her mind went to details.

His mouth curled at the corner. "It's already dying out. I adjusted the damper earlier, so it'll burn down."

Owen reached the bottom of the spiral staircase and adjusted her in his arms. In moments, he reached the top, nudging a light switch with his elbow. Low lights came on overhead. Ivy glanced around, taking in the room. His bedroom occupied most of the floor up here. A large bed was built into the curved wall on one side with a fluffy down quilt and mounds of pillows. A dresser curved along another part of the wall with two inviting chairs in dove gray fabric facing the windows. It was dark outside, so she couldn't see, but she guessed the windows offered a view of the bay. He walked past the bed and to a door on the other side. Lights came on automatically as he shouldered through. The bathroom had a massive tiled shower in the corner and a lovely oval shaped tub on the other side with sinks in between.

He carried her into the shower, tossing the blanket to the floor as they stepped through. Hot water appeared as if by magic. Ivy's engineer brain realized he must have a system direct to this shower that was motion activated, as the lights were. In seconds, she was standing under the scalding hot water with his hands sliding soap over her skin. His touch was practical and soothing at once. He was quiet, and she didn't want to talk either. All she wanted was to enjoy every minute of this. When he soaped between her thighs, she felt a subtle sting. His eyes flicked to hers. "Okay?"

"Uh huh," she managed. "Just a little sore."

A flush of embarrassment rose within. Losing her virginity definitely wasn't like learning to drive. His seemed to sense her reluctance for further talk and nodded. Moments later, he handed her a fluffy towel and she dried off. This was the part she hadn't considered. She'd had this crazy idea they'd do this thing and then it would be over, and the wild, pounding need he drew from her would be sated for once and for all. The satiation was fleeting, and the intimacy of tonight hung around them.

As she stood there wondering what to do, he saved her by curling his hand around hers and tugging her to his bed. He lifted the blanket above them, cool air rushing over her skin as it drifted down. A chill raced through her, but he curled on his side and tugged her firmly against him. His heat immediately warmed her. With her body humming still from the pleasure he wrought, she slowly fell asleep.

CHAPTER 10

Owen strode quickly down the hallway at Off the Grid. As he passed by Derek's office, he heard his name and came to an abrupt stop. He took a few steps back and leaned through Derek's doorway. "Yeah?"

"Any word on the status of the project we sent to assembly?" Derek asked.

"Yup. Should have a prototype ready by next week."

Derek nodded quickly. "Got it."

When he didn't say anything else, Owen couldn't help but ask, "Anything else?"

Derek glanced from his computer screen back up to Owen. "Nah. I was actually wondering about that, but more curious to see if you were paying attention."

Owen took another step into Derek's office and crossed his arms over his chest. "And why's that?"

"Because you've been half out of it for days now. You're getting plenty done, but not paying much attention to anyone. What gives?"

Owen beat back the annoyance rising inside. Derek was on point, and Owen knew precisely why. Ever since he'd gone completely mad and decided there was some chance he could get Ivy out of his system, he'd been facing the brutal truth that he was now at the mercy of the wild, powerful connection between them. He'd been stupid enough to think perhaps a few nights with her would flush the pounding need for her clear out of him. Instead, he'd hardly been able to stop thinking about her since the other night. Even worse, the idea that they were somehow going to move past what happened to a platonic, collegial friendship was ridiculous. Simply thinking about it made him angry. Because if there was one thing he knew now, all he wanted was *more*.

More of her dewy skin, her abandoned response to him, the feel of her channel clenching around him, her lips under his, the amber fire of her eyes flashing...and hours and hours of engineer-speak. God, he loved talking to her. She was flat brilliant and so damn passionate about her research. It was like intellectual sex, definitely a first for him, just as the other night was the first time he'd experienced sex that went beyond the physical—a melding of body and mind. The fleeting concerns he'd dismissed beforehand—the logistical concern about her virginity and the practical concern about how to graciously get past any awkwardness—had turned out to be inconsequential. However, he'd completely underestimated what it would be like to actually be skin to skin with her, to feel the depth of connection between them beating as if it had a heart of its own.

Back to Derek's point. Yeah, Owen was distracted. He'd thrown himself into work the last few days and knew he might be coming across as snappy at points. Work was his refuge. Complicating his distracted state further was Ivy's presence at Off the Grid. He was being scrupulously polite and constantly fighting, full on internal battles, with himself to keep from slamming the door to her office and taking her against the wall, on the table, against the windows and so on. His mind spun back to the other morning and waking up beside her. He tended to sleep lightly, yet falling asleep with Ivy's luscious body curled up against him had been a heaven he'd never imagined. He'd slept so deeply, he'd been disoriented when he woke. His body hadn't been the least bit disoriented as he woke up rock hard and ready for more.

Derek cleared his throat, and Owen realized he'd been standing there zoning out. What the hell had Derek asked? Oh right, he wanted to know why Owen was so distracted. Startling himself, he was completely honest. "It's Ivy."

Derek arched a brow and turned fully away from his computer. Being the good friend he was, he didn't tease just now. He nodded to the door behind Owen. "Close the door," he said.

Owen reached behind him and gave the door a push, just enough for it to swing shut. He walked to Derek's worktable and sat down in the chair across from Derek, running a hand through his hair and leaning back.

Owen wished Derek could save him from trying to stumble through how to explain the mess in his brain. Instead, Derek went straight to the heart of the matter. "Right. Ivy. What about Ivy?"

Owen angled his head to the side and rolled his eyes. "Isn't it enough I admitted it? What do I need to explain?"

Derek cracked a laugh, his grin fading quickly when he saw the pained expression on Owen's face. "Okay, fine. I guessed right. You like her. No need to go into the gory details, but what's the problem? I'm not all about romance, but if there was ever a woman perfect for you, it's Ivy Nash."

Owen leaned his head back with a sigh. "The problem is she makes me crazy. I don't like being distracted like this. I don't know what the hell to do about her and..." His words ran out, and he shook his head.

Derek was quiet for a few beats. He angled his head to the side, idly twirling a pencil between his fingers. "Your work doesn't seem to be affected, if anything, you're like a madman. It's just you're a bit cranky with everyone around you. Maybe you should stop thinking so damn much about it. You like her. Go with it."

"Go with it?"

Derek nodded. "Yup. For once in your life, stop trying to compartmentalize everything personal. Far as I can tell, Ivy's in as bad as you. It's kinda funny how you both just bury yourselves in research as an escape. I'm not even trying to be funny. I've known you long enough to know what I see. You like her, and she likes you. Stop worrying about keeping it clean. Maybe you'll be better off if you let some steam off anyway."

Owen stared at Derek for a long moment before shrugging. "I'll take that on advisement."

Derek chuckled. "Do that. Try being nicer to everyone while you're at it."

Owen pushed back his chair and stood, managing to laugh for the first time in a few days. "Working on it," he said over his shoulder as he exited Derek's office.

Instead of heading to wherever the hell he'd been going, and damn if he could recall, he turned back in the direction where he'd come from and stopped in front of Ivy's office. She was angled away from the door, her hair tied up in another loose knot atop her head. He rapped lightly on the glass door and opened it as soon as she glanced over and waved him in. He locked the door behind him and tapped the button that levered the vertical blinds over the glass closed. Ivy spun in her chair, her eyes widening slightly. This was the first time since the weekend that he'd allowed himself to be alone with her because being alone with her was downright dangerous.

She wore a bulky red sweater over a pair of leggings. As

he'd come to learn was common, she'd kicked her boots off, and they lay on the floor by her worktable. Her socks were bright red to match her sweater. For some reason, this small detail made his heart squeeze. He walked straight to her and leaned over, his hands resting on the arms of her chair. Getting this close fuzzed his brain, the scent of her wafted over him. He could see her pulse fluttering in her neck. He forced himself to hold still for a moment. The moment immediately got shorter when she bit her lip—the sight of her teeth denting the plump cushion of her bottom lip undid him. He carefully took her glasses off and set them on the table before dipping his head and kissing her.

Kiss didn't quite capture what passed between them— scalding hot, raw need poured through him when her tongue slid sensuously against his. He yanked back, searching her eyes. She closed them and swallowed.

"I can't think when you do that," she whispered into the silence loaded with the weight of their need. "You've hardly talked to me and I don't know..."

"I know. I'm sorry. This isn't what I thought it would be." His rough whispered reply startled him. This was the second time today he'd shocked himself with his honesty.

She opened her eyes, meeting his. "What do you mean?"

"I don't really know, but I know I don't want to keep trying to steer clear of you. I want..." He paused, trying to clarify what it was that he wanted. "You."

The single word fell into the space between them. Her eyes widened and her breath came in short pants. "Does that mean you're going to hardly talk to me anymore?"

He shook his head. He didn't know what the hell he was doing, but trying to keep her in a corner in his mind was hell. He was going to take Derek's advice, not because of Derek, but because it felt right. "No. I think it's better if I stop avoiding what I want."

She swallowed again, her tongue darting out to lick her lips. "Okay. So what does that mean?"

"This." He leaned closer and curled his hand around her hips, lifting her up into his arms and against him. Her legs reflexively wrapped around his hips, and he gloried in the feel of her heat against his cock. Every second he was near her, he was fighting an erection. It was pure relief to stop worrying about it. With the wall conveniently right there, he spun around and eased her back against the wall before diving into another kiss.

He poured everything into her mouth—the pent up need burning and yearning inside of him. She didn't hold back, throwing herself into their kiss, which got rougher and hotter with every stroke and nip. He pulled back and shoved her sweater up, grinning at the sight of her barely there bra. She was so practical when it came to her clothes, he loved that no one would guess her tendency toward sheer lace lingerie that was so decadent it hardly passed for doing its job. With one hand gripping her hip and holding her in place against him, he used the other to trace circles around the tight peaks of her nipples, rolling them between his thumb and forefinger and reveling in her soft gasps. He yanked her sweater over her head and flicked the clasp between her breasts, groaning at the sight of her pink nipples. He let the reins loosen more when he dipped his head and drew one and then the other into his mouth, biting down softly before he pulled back.

"Owen, we can't…"

"Can't what?"

"We're in the office and it's the middle of the day!" she whispered fiercely, her cheeks stained with a pink flush.

He was so far gone, he truly didn't give a damn. But he wasn't stupid either. "I didn't just close the blinds. I locked the door. Hardly anyone comes down here anyway. As far as everyone knows, my schedule says I'm tied up on a conference call."

Her eyes stared back at him. He could practically see her fighting with herself. "Well, shouldn't you be on the conference call then?" she asked, biting her lip again.

He couldn't help but arch into the warm shelter of her hips, his cock hardening further at the feel of her damp heat against him. He shook his head. "No, I shouldn't. I can hardly think. I just need a little of…" He paused and dragged his thumb back and forth over a nipple before sliding it down over the curve of her belly, under the waistband of her leggings and over the damp silk of her panties. "…this. Then, maybe I can think straight."

Her eyes fell closed on a moan as he dragged a finger back and forth over the silk, before shoving it out of the way and delving into her folds. Her head fell against the wall as he slid one finger and then another into her channel. She was so wet, he almost came at the feel of her on his fingers. Within seconds, her channel was clenching with her hips rolling into his touch. He could sense she was holding back.

"Ivy," he whispered roughly.

Those gorgeous eyes opened, her lids at half-mast.

"Just let it happen."

He swirled his thumb over her clit with the next surge of his fingers, and she bit her lip as she cried out, her head falling to the wall again.

* * *

IVY DRAGGED her eyes open to find Owen's bright blue gaze waiting for her. She'd gone and lost her mind, letting him drive her wild with his fingers in her office like that. *In her office!* Part of her thought she should be mortified, but under the warmth of his gaze, she didn't feel anything other than satisfied. He slowly slipped his hand out and eased her down. When he stepped away, she sensed he intended for her to be the only one who walked away from this with release. She was finding Owen made her greedy. She wanted more, and she wanted him to find the same satisfaction she just had. She reached for him, swiftly unbuttoning his jeans and sliding her hand inside.

"Ivy, you don't have…"

"Oh shut up." She felt emboldened and reckless, a feeling she was coming to associate solely with Owen.

She curled her palm around the heated length of him before shoving his jeans and briefs down, just far enough to free him. Before he had a chance to say anything else, she spun around, pushing him against the wall and leaning forward to take him in her mouth. He groaned, and she grinned when she heard his head slam against the wall behind him. She savored the silky feel of his skin under her tongue as she explored him. He gripped her hair as she settled in—alternating between bringing him into her mouth, curling her fist around his length and exploring every inch of him with her tongue. He tasted sweet and salty, and she wanted more. She felt her channel clenching in response to his low groans. She took him deeper into her mouth and settled into a rhythm with her palm curled loosely around him. With a growl, he gripped her hair as his body went taut, his release spurting into her mouth. She slowly drew back and looked up at him.

He lifted his head and stared down at her. The air between them tightened, the same powerful wash of intimacy she'd felt with him the other night shimmering around them. She almost couldn't bear it and broke away from his gaze as she slowly stood. Surprising her, he pulled her close to him, brushing her hair, which had fallen loose in the midst of this madness, away from her face. He leaned his forehead to hers. "Thank you," he said, his voice gruff.

She leaned back. "I think I'm supposed to thank you first."

He chuckled and shook his head. "I guess I didn't expect that."

"I didn't expect any of this, so…"

He closed his eyes for a moment. When he opened them again, she couldn't quite read his gaze.

"I suppose we should get back to work," she finally said.

He nodded slowly, easing his hold on her waist. They tugged their clothes back into place. She started to tie her hair up, pausing at the sound of his voice.

"Leave it down," he said.

When she stared blankly at him, he spoke again. "Please."

Uncertain how to respond, she dropped her hands and sifted them through her hair, tidying it. He walked to the door and paused beside it.

"Can we have dinner again?" he asked.

She nodded before she even thought about his question. Because, the truth was, she couldn't even fathom saying no to anything he asked.

CHAPTER 11

*I*vy nearly jumped out of her chair when George bounced into her lap from the windowsill. "George! You startled me!" she exclaimed as she glanced down to pet him.

Ginger laughed from over by the refrigerator where she was putting away groceries. "He still scares me sometimes. He'll be hanging out chillin' and all the sudden, he's in my lap."

Ivy stroked George's silky gray ears as he settled into her lap. "How was your day?" she asked.

Ginger had arrived home a few minutes behind her. Ivy had just finished helping her lug groceries in from her car. Ginger closed the refrigerator and lifted her hands to brush her hair away from her face and pull it into a knot. She sat down across from Ivy with a sigh. "Long. We had student planning meetings all day today."

"Oh, how often do you have to do those?"

Ginger shrugged. "Once a year unless something needs to be tweaked. Since I'm the only speech therapist at the school, if a student gets speech therapy, I'm involved. After today, I only have a few annuals left. Anyway, enough about me. How about you? What's up at Off the Grid?"

Ivy's mind flashed to the last few days, and heat rolled through her. Ever since Owen had nearly melted her into a puddle in her office the other day, things had been much better between them. The simmering tension was still present, but there was an outlet now. They'd yet to have the dinner he'd asked her about, but she hadn't really thought about it. Stolen kisses were getting her through her days.

Ginger's snort brought Ivy back to the moment. She looked up to find Ginger grinning. "Well, I don't know what's going on, but I'm guessing after your night with Owen last weekend, things are a tad less tense around the office."

Since she was staying with Ginger and Cam, Ivy had felt like she had to tell them she had plans last weekend. She hadn't wanted to get into the details with Cam, so she'd sworn Ginger to secrecy. Ivy met Ginger's laughing gaze with a shrug and a flush. "They are. Anyway, work is great. I'm learning to love how much flexibility we have there. We have a prototype assembly team on site, so whenever we think a design is ready to test, it's sent out right away. I've already gotten to see the results for some modifications I suggested on the battery project."

Ginger was gracious enough to ask a few questions and before Ivy knew it, she was carrying on about technical details. She looked over to see Ginger's eyes glazing over and stopped mid-sentence. "I'm sorry," she said with a rueful smile. "I get caught up when I'm talking about stuff like this. I know it can be a little boring for most people."

Ginger laughed softly as she stood and turned on the oven. She pulled a bottle of wine off the rack on the wall before grabbing two wineglasses and carrying them to the table. "I admit I lose track of the details, mostly because it's way above my head. I bet Owen follows along just fine," she said with a wink as she poured Ivy a glass of wine and spun back to put a casserole pan in the oven.

Ivy couldn't help but smile at Ginger's comment. Talking to Owen was like foreplay and not because they were actually flirting. She took a sip of wine and watched while Ginger puttered around the kitchen, prepping a salad and checking on the casserole. Ginger and Cam had acquiesced to Ivy's offer to take care of cleaning and laundry every weekend. Ginger waved her away whenever Ivy offered to make dinner. Ivy considered herself a serviceable cook, but Ginger's cooking was sublime, so Ivy figured it was a win for all of them. Ivy's phone buzzed on the table. She picked it up and answered it, carefully sliding George off her lap as she stepped out of the kitchen.

"Hello?"

"Hello Ivy."

Dr. Parkhurst's voice was instantly recognizable. She'd liked to have forgotten the sound of his voice, but she hadn't. Her stomach coiled with dread. She forced herself to take a deep breath and considered hanging up. She wouldn't cower though. It had taken all of her nerve to report his harassment. Now that she was no longer under his thumb, she wasn't going to let him scare her.

"You're not supposed to contact me," she said flatly.

"Ah, Ivy." He actually tsk-tsked her before continuing. "This is simply a friendly phone call, an olive branch. I'm sorry for the misunderstandings between us and wanted to call and wish you well. I hear great things about your work at Owen Manning's firm."

Her mind spun. She didn't know what Dr. Parkhurst wanted out of contacting her, but it was something. It wouldn't surprise her to learn he hoped to connect himself to Off the Grid somehow. It would be a channel of funding and projects he could tag his name onto. Even though Dr. Parkhurst's position was secure, his arrogance and need for attention was endless. Ivy took another slow breath and reminded herself the less she interacted with him, the better. "I'll reiterate: you're not supposed to contact me. There's an active investigation. Please don't call me."

At that, she pulled her phone away and tapped the screen closed. Her heart was pounding and not in the good way. She'd forgotten the sick anxiety and tension he elicited. She'd lived with it for a year before deciding she couldn't tolerate it anymore. She walked to the windows looking out over the bay, her arms wrapped across her waist. She concentrated on breathing slowly as she stared out over the water. The days were gradually lengthening. The transition from the dark days of winter to spring here in Alaska was more dramatic than in Utah. However, both places shared the sense of burgeoning energy as the darkness of winter was overtaken by light. Snow still covered the peaks of the mountains across the water and the air was cold every day, but Ivy could feel spring coming. A raven called from a tree on the bluff behind the house, another raven returning the call. The sun was falling down the sky, about to slip behind the mountains, leaving a watercolor of pink and lavender in its wake.

Her heart slowly eased its nervous pounding, and she managed to take several deep breaths, yet her stomach held onto the sick feeling. Dr. Parkhurst made her feel yucky. That was the only word she could come up with. With another deep breath, she returned to the kitchen. Ginger was in the middle of opening the oven to put in a loaf of buttered garlic bread. She closed it and turned as Ivy was sitting down. Much as Ivy wished she could mask the expression on her face, she couldn't muster it just now.

"Are you okay?" Ginger asked, her eyes scanning Ivy's face as tossed the oven mitt on the counter and sat down across from Ivy.

Ivy tried to shrug and smile, but it wobbled. She grabbed

her wineglass and took a gulp. "That was Dr. Parkhurst. I swear, if I never hear that man's voice again, I'll be happy."

Ginger's eyes widened. "What the hell? What did he want?"

Ivy shrugged. "I have no idea. He said something about an olive branch and hearing great things about my work with Owen." She leaned her head in her hands and closed her eyes. "He makes me so sick. I hate that he can still get to me, and I feel so stupid. I mean, he was nothing more than a creepy jerk, but he was always throwing his weight around and dropping hints about how he could make or break my career." She lifted her head and took another sip of wine. "What if he tries to mess things up here for me?"

Ginger's eyes were practically shooting knives. "No! He can't touch you here. He's just being shitty and trying to fix things. Call HR at the university and tell them he contacted you. He's not even supposed to call, right?"

Ivy shrugged. "I don't know. I mean, when I was officially employed there, once I filed the complaint, he was under orders not to contact me. It was horrible trying to work knowing he was nearby. I don't get how it works now that I left. They told me as long as the investigation was active, he's supposed to leave me alone, but it's not like it really matters. This is just a stupid HR complaint, nothing criminal." She gave her head a sharp shake. "I can't even think about him. I moved on."

Ginger's eyes coasted over her, and she reached across the table to squeeze Ivy's hand. "You did. You're long gone from there, and you don't need to worry about him. Promise me you'll let us know if he keeps calling."

Ivy swallowed against the tight feeling in her chest and nodded. "I will."

Ginger released her hand and leaned back in her chair. "Just remember you don't need to worry about him anymore. Okay?"

Ivy managed a nod, but she still felt slightly queasy. She was relieved when the front door opened at that moment and Cam stepped through. George bounced from his perch by the window to Cam's feet, and Ginger spun in her chair to call out a greeting.

Later that night, Ivy curled on her side and looked out into the darkness. Stars glittered in the sky. Clouds drifted in front of the moon, smudging the light falling across the water. She couldn't shake her restlessness and rolled over onto her back, staring at the dark ceiling. With a sigh, she fumbled on the nightstand and grabbed her phone. Propping herself up on the pillows, she started playing a word game. She'd been out of sorts ever since that stupid phone call earlier. Once she'd gotten over the sick feeling, she'd swung to anger. When she managed to stop dwelling on that, she wanted to see Owen, which made her feel unsettled and vulnerable.

This whole *thing* they were doing was supposed to be neat and tidy, compartmentalized to sex and burning out the crazy hot chemistry between them. It wasn't supposed to include her wishing she could hear his voice because he made her smile and somehow made her feel protected. Not that she needed protecting from anyone, but Dr. Parkhurst had spent over a year threatening her career if she didn't give into what he wanted. Finally getting out from under his thumb had been such a relief, she forgot how bad it felt. No matter what Ginger said, Dr. Parkhurst still could make things difficult for her in the field. He had too much influence in the field of engineering and more specifically in the realm of sustainable energy. He might not be able to get her fired or interfere with her work directly, but he could drop a few hints here and there and create questions about her work.

Ivy kept playing her word game and fighting the urge to text Owen. After a few more minutes, she swore and gave in. He probably wasn't even awake, so it wouldn't even matter.

Hey.

She'd keep it basic, so he wouldn't think she was being weird if he were even awake to read it. Before she switched back to the game screen, her phone vibrated in her hand.

Hey there. Shouldn't you be asleep?

She smiled and wiggled her toes.

Maybe, but I'm not. Shouldn't you be asleep?

She could see his smile right now. Just thinking about the corner of his mouth curling up sent flutters spinning in her belly.

I'm usually up late working. You?

She thought about saying she was working, but she didn't really feel like it.

Can't sleep. Playing Spellsage instead.

Ah. Good to know your word game of choice. I'm a fan too. You okay?

Shrug. Just some stuff.

Stuff?

Too much to explain in a text.

Hmm. Later?

Maybe. Anyway, how r u? Too busy this afternoon to say hi.

She'd been tied up in a planning meeting with the battery team, while Owen had been holed up in his office with Derek. Owen had been true to his word and eased away from leading the battery project team once she had a good sense of where they were at with the various designs. As such, she didn't encounter him as often throughout the day.

I'll stop in first thing tomorrow.

Okay.

She sat there, wondering what else to say and feeling kind of silly.

'Spose you should try to get some sleep?

That's the idea. Not so sure Spellsage will do the trick.

I know what would.

Four simple words, and she squeezed her knees together, trying to quell the throb of desire. It was getting ridiculous how easily he affected her. They'd only had one night together, and it appeared to have made things far worse.

That would definitely do the trick. Too bad we can't do anything about it.

Sure we can. Tell me how wet you are.

Ivy's eyes widened, and she gasped, reflexively glancing around as if someone might notice. She was alone in the darkness of her bedroom with nothing but the stars to see. She stared at his words. Her pulse raced, her belly clenched, and she was drenched. She couldn't quite believe it, but she couldn't reel herself in and stop this.

Very.

Good. Take your panties off.

She didn't even consider not obeying and quickly lifted her hips and shimmied out of her panties, kicking them to the side under the covers. He beat her to her reply.

Okay, now lick one finger for me.

Not an ounce of hesitation from her. She drew her forefinger into her mouth and swirled her tongue around it, imagining the feel of his hard cock in her mouth as she did.

He seemed to be tracking the time, just the thing he would do.

Now, drag it back and forth. You know where.

With her heart beating wildly and searing need gripping her, she dragged her finger back and forth through her folds. She was so wet, it had been entirely unnecessary for her to bother with anything else. Her hips bucked into her hand. Just as she was about to slide her finger into her channel, her phone buzzed. She dragged her eyes open and looked down.

Not yet. Spread your knees wider. Tell me how wet you are.

With her knees splayed wide and teetering on the edge of an orgasm, she managed to type a reply with one hand.

Soaked. Can't keep waiting.

She could feel his grin—a dark, naughty grin.

Fine. One finger inside.

She bit her lip to keep from crying out. Her channel throbbed around her finger as she stroked in and out. With her phone resting on her low belly, she felt the vibration of it when he sent another message. She looked down.

Another.

Obedient again, she let a second finger join the first, a low moan escaping when she did. Her hips were rolling into her hand, and she could see his bright blue eyes in her mind and recall the feel of him stretching and filling her. Her phone buzzed again.

Now.

She gave in, pressed her thumb over her clit and cried out, her channel clenching around her fingers. Her head fell back against the pillows, her breath coming in deep gusts. Her body slowly relaxed and a smile spread across her face. Her phone buzzed again, and she picked it up.

Sleep tight.

CHAPTER 12

Owen stood in front of the windows in his office, yet again staring out over the view. The sky, mountains and water offered shades of gray this morning. He'd come in early, not unusual for him. Ivy's late night text message had caught him at a weak moment. Well, if he was being honest, anything to do with her made him weak. He'd had to find his own release last night, a purely practical matter. He'd awoken this morning, rock hard with need and Ivy on the brain. Refusing to give in again because he knew it wouldn't satiate him, he'd showered and driven the short distance to the office.

He was restless and irritable and couldn't stop looking through his door, wondering when he'd see her walking down the hallway. With a muttered curse, he turned away from the window and forced himself to try to focus. He managed to get through a few emails from Joan about finances and the mundane details about changes to the company's health plan offering when he heard footsteps coming down the tiled hallway. A glance up gave him a view of Derek striding toward his office. He swatted away the disappointment he felt at not seeing Ivy and waved Derek into his office.

Derek immediately strode to his worktable and spun a computer screen around. He wasn't one to bother with preliminaries when he wanted to work. Within moments, they were deep into a discussion about data coming in from various test designs. Owen finally managed to get his mind off of Ivy. The morning passed quickly between his meeting with Derek, Joan stopping by and forcing him to review the health plan information and several calls from the assembly team. After hanging up the phone from another call, he glanced up at the clock above his door to find it was close to noon, and he hadn't seen Ivy yet.

The moment she strolled into his thoughts, he had to see her. He walked quickly to her office and saw it was empty. Her coat was thrown on the back of her chair, so he figured she was somewhere in the building. He actually had to order himself not to go looking for her. His grand plan to keep his out-of-control, raging lust for her in a tidy corner of his life wasn't working out so well. He spun on his heel and returned to his office. He could spend all day plowing through emails, which he usually avoided. For now, it seemed like the perfect activity to keep him occupied. As he cruised through, responding and deleting the wall of emails, something clicked in the back of his mind when he saw an email address for the engineering program where Ivy had done her doctoral work and stayed on the faculty afterwards.

He scrolled down and clicked on the email. It had been sent yesterday and was from Dr. Parkhurst. Owen knew Dr. Parkhurst in passing, and he'd found him to be grating in person. He'd been a lead engineer on some of the original solar designs back in the early days of development and remained a leader in the field, although he hadn't conducted or published any new research in over a decade. In the field of engineering, that was a damn long time. He still held sway mostly because he made a show of himself at various annual conferences. Owen scanned the email, Ivy's name jumping out as if it had been typed in neon. Dr. Parkhurst was inquiring as to how Ivy was adjusting and offering consultation to Off the Grid if needed.

A few sentences made Owen want to punch the man. "Ms. Nash is quite brilliant, but she has yet to develop the confidence she needs. Without my support, it's not likely her research papers would have passed muster. I'd be happy to consult on projects with her as needed if you find she could use additional expertise." Owen read the words several times, his blood pressure rising with each pass. He fought the urge to type a dismissive reply. What the hell was Parkhurst after? Owen's mind spun back to the comment Cam had made about the chair at Ivy's department being an old creeper. He was familiar with Parkhurst, but didn't know his actual role on the faculty. He quickly looked it up, his stomach clenching with anger to see Parkhurst listed as the Engineering Department Chair. Dear God. The man was old enough to be Ivy's father and potentially her grandfather, and he was the jerk who went after her.

He was seething inside and stood abruptly. He started to move toward Ivy's office again and forced himself to stop. What the hell could he say to her about this? She hadn't shared any of this with him and was likely beyond relieved to have left Parkhurst in the dust. An intense need to protect her, to make sure she knew he wouldn't let Parkhurst anywhere near her or her career, and to somehow make amends for the whole shitty situation rose within him. He turned to the windows again, staring out into the gray day, the foreboding sky a match for his mood. It looked like snow was on the way.

He stared out for several moments, pondering what he could do to make Parkhurst pay and to get him to back the hell off once and for all. He mostly came up empty at the moment because everything he wanted involved punching Parkhurst in the face. While Owen wasn't above that, he knew Ivy wouldn't appreciate the attention that might draw. Not to mention, Parkhurst was thousands of miles away. Much as he itched to type a blistering reply about how little Ivy needed anyone's support for her research, he knew the most stinging response for Parkhurst would be none. Not because of him hoping to link himself to Ivy again somehow, but because it would chafe at him to be ignored by Owen. He sought adulation from other engineers who had any publicity attached to them. Owen didn't put much stock in public attention, but he knew he had it, so it would bite Parkhurst for him to not even bother with a reply.

Bottling up his anger, he stalked out of his office only to come to a screeching halt when he saw Ivy sitting at her desk. She had her phone to her ear as she fiddled with the silver bracelets on her wrist. He'd noticed she did that when she was nervous. She'd yet to see him standing outside her door. Tension lined her face. He couldn't help himself and rapped quickly on the door before stepping inside. Her eyes flicked to him and then to the wall. She was gripping the phone so hard, her knuckles were white. She spun her chair away from him.

"Dr. Parkhurst, please don't..."

She paused, appearing to react to an interruption. The anger Owen had barely stuffed flared fast and hot. He stalked to her side and reached to grab the phone, only stopping when he realized she probably wouldn't appreciate him going all manly on her. Barely leashing his anger, he tapped her shoulder and held out his hand. She shook her head and barked into the phone. "Do. Not. Call. Me. Again." She threw the phone on the table where it slid across the surface and clattered onto the floor by his feet. He picked it up and set it carefully on the table, checking to make sure the call had ended first.

Spinning her chair away, she put her face in her hands, her shoulders curling inward. She breathed in deep gulps of air and was otherwise silent. He remained where he was, once again trying to swallow his anger and uncertain how to help her. Everything about her body language screamed that she didn't want to be touched. No matter how much he wanted to yank her into his arms, he didn't. Instead, he sank down into one of the chairs by the windows and waited.

After a few minutes, Ivy lifted her head and slid her hands through her hair. She slowly spun her chair around to face him. Her eyes were red and her cheeks blotchy. His heart clenched, but he waited.

She lifted her hand as if she was about to gesture, but she let it drop into her lap. "I, uh…" She closed her eyes and leaned her head back. When she opened them again, she straightened her shoulders. "I guess I should tell you what that was about." The look of trepidation on her face almost caused him physical pain. He considered it was probably better if he let her know what he knew, rather than trying to play it like he had no idea. He'd only put the pieces together today, so he didn't feel as if he'd been hiding something.

"Ivy?"

She'd taken up fiddling with her bracelets again. "Yeah?"

"I might have an idea what that was about."

"What do you mean?"

"I didn't think much of it at the time, but your brother mentioned something about an 'old creeper' making life miserable for you at the university. It made me sick to hear it, but it's not like I don't know how often crap like that happens. That was before…" He paused to clear his throat, not quite sure how to label what was happening between them. "Before anything happened with us. Anyway, this morning I started going through my emails and came across one Dr. Parkhurst sent yesterday. He offered to consult on your work if I thought we needed it. The fact he even offered is a joke, but I put the pieces together and figured out he must be the jerk Cam mentioned."

He watched Ivy, seeing a mix of emotions pass through her amber eyes. Her shoulders sank in resignation, and she looked weary. "I should've told you. I just…"

Owen shook his head quickly. "You didn't have to tell me any of it. Parkhurst is a scumbag. I'd like to say his behavior surprises me, but it doesn't. In addition to being rigid and moving at the pace of a snail, university environments are full of old geezers who ogle grad students and young faculty all the time. Far as I'm concerned, it's a damn good thing you left. Too bad you didn't find Off the Grid sooner. Aside from dodging handsy department chairs, you're too damn smart to be held back like you would've been there."

He was battling a storm of feelings—anger and disgust with Parkhurst, frustration and sadness at the situation Ivy had been thrust into, and an intense need to wrap her in his arms. A look of relief passed across her face as she took a deep breath and straightened her shoulders again.

"Why was Parkhurst calling you?" he asked.

"I don't know. He called yesterday and said something about apologizing for any misunderstandings between us. I told him he wasn't supposed to call me. Because he's not. I filed a formal complaint before I left, and that's when things got really awful. I don't know for sure, but rumor has it he's pulled this crap for years and the complaints never go anywhere. It was like he was determined to wear me down. No matter what I did, he could make it nearly impossible for me to advance there, so I decided to cut my losses. I honestly don't know what he thinks he can get from calling me now. Maybe he thinks I'll drop my complaint, maybe he thinks he can make things difficult for me here. I don't know." She kept twisting her bracelets. She bit her lip and looked over at him.

"Anything he thinks he can do, he can't," Owen said flatly. "It's easy to forget when you're mired in academia, but many of the higher ups there aren't as powerful as they like to think. Parkhurst is washed up and hasn't done anything productive in the field for years. I'm sure he made things damn miserable for you there, but he can't anywhere else. If he tries to pull any bullshit, I'll make sure he regrets it."

Before he realized he was moving, he stood and took the few strides to reach her, curling his hands around hers as he leaned forward. "You already put him behind you no matter what he thinks. If he calls you again, let me know."

Ivy's hands were ice cold in his. He held on, trying to impart his heat to her. She didn't pull away and gave a return squeeze, though her eyes retained the worry held there. "I will. It's just all so frustrating. I hate that he can still get to me like this."

"It might feel like he can, but he can't."

At Ivy's nod, he gave her hands a tug. "Come on. Let's go grab that dinner I asked you about."

"But it's early and…"

"You work late all the time. Let's go." He gave another tug and she stood, giving the first hint of a smile he'd seen since he walked into her office in the middle of her tense call with Parkhurst.

When she began to put her coat on, he stepped into his office to power everything down and grab his jacket. As they walked outside, the snow he'd guessed was on its way had started to fall.

Ivy turned her face to the sky, a smile curling her lips. "Almost spring snow!"

He couldn't help but chuckle. "There's not really a spring in Alaska, it's more like a day or two and then it's summer."

She started to walk toward her car, so he grabbed her hand. "Ride with me. No need for you to drive."

She spun to face him, her amber eyes bright in the wispy light of early evening with the snow falling around her like fairy dust. "Okay. Where are we going?"

"Your choice."

She cocked her head to the side and bit her lip again, something he noticed she did when she was pondering and something that made him hard almost every time she did it. "Would you mind if we went to the lodge restaurant? Ginger and Cam will be there, and I just kinda want to be around my friends right now."

Normally, Owen's answer would be a definitive no. He wasn't much for social gatherings, no matter how casual. But he couldn't say no to Ivy, and he was coming to understand what Cam had said about her. She naturally leaned toward others, both giving and seeking support. Beyond quickly earning universal respect among the team of engineers at Off the Grid, she'd also endeared herself to the office staff by making coffee every day and easily taking care of mundane tasks often avoided by the other engineers.

So, he nodded and held open the passenger door for her.

CHAPTER 13

Ivy rolled over and collided with a warm, muscled body, the delicious heat nudging her into awareness. Owen's muscled arm was draped over her waist as she turned in his sleepy embrace. She relaxed against his side, sliding her foot up along his calf. Last night had been layers of amazing—hot, body melting amazing. After the unsettling call from Dr. Parkhurst, she'd had mixed feelings about learning Owen had pieced the details together. She'd managed to put her worries about it away, at least for the night. She'd sensed Owen hadn't been too thrilled when she suggested dinner at the lodge, but he'd gamely gone along. It had been beyond good to relax with Cam and Ginger and their mixed group of friends who rotated by the table. Ivy hadn't planned it that way, but it was nice to see Owen letting down his guard more. The man she'd come to know was reserved. The bits and pieces she'd learned of his past helped her understand why he kept his distance, but it worried her that he didn't allow himself to be closer to others. She couldn't say she knew what it was like to lose two parents in one swoop, but she knew what a painful loss was like. What had healed her was to pull those she loved closer.

She opened her eyes. He was sound asleep, his chest rising and falling in steady, even breaths. His features were softer in sleep. She fought the urge to trace a finger along his stubbled jaw. After dinner, he'd brought her home with him and proceeded to drive her completely wild. Just thinking about it sent a wash of heat through her. She closed her eyes and tried to steady her pulse. She didn't quite know what to do with what was happening with Owen. She couldn't say she'd known how it would play out because she'd never done anything like this. She thought she'd manage to leave her virginity behind her and that it wouldn't be too hard to burn out the scorching flames of their attraction.

It didn't seem to be working out that way. If anything, every time she was with Owen, the burning longing inside grew and got bolder. She'd expected him to keep his distance at work, but he wasn't. Oh, when it came to the actual work, he left her to her own devices. She was busy with her projects, while he was busy with whatever he was working on. He had his fingertips on everything at Off the Grid, but he was heavily focused on only a few projects. Yet, beyond the 'work' at work, he was surprising her with the frequency with which he sought her out. Case in point, when he popped in her office the other afternoon and left her nearly boneless after making her see stars.

Just thinking about those heated moments, her belly did a slow flip and she clenched her thighs together. He shifted in his sleep and mumbled something. She gave into the urge to open her eyes again, this time letting her hand stroke across his chest. He opened his eyes, his gaze immediately locking with hers. Holy hell. His blue eyes were dangerous all on their own, but hooded and sleepy...well, they sent a sizzling zing through her insides. In a flash, he sat up and hauled her into his arms, striding to the shower.

A while later, she tugged on her clothes and made her way down the spiral staircase. She found Owen busy in the kitchen making omelets. He nudged his chin in the direction of the coffee pot when she approached the kitchen counter. "Forgot to start coffee, but then I thought you wouldn't mind making it."

"Of course. Where…?"

"Coffee beans are in the cabinet above it," he said, reading her mind.

After a leisurely breakfast, Owen returned her to her car. It was Saturday, so the parking lot at Off the Grid was mostly empty. Ivy couldn't help but wonder who might be working. She wanted to ask Owen what he was doing, but that wasn't what they did. Although she didn't think what they did last night fell into the idea of what Owen had originally proposed either. That unsettling thought prompted her to wave casually and jump in her car. She'd find a way to think about something other than Owen for the rest of the day.

* * *

OWEN TRIED to bury himself in work for most of Saturday morning, but he was restless and constantly had to swat thoughts of Ivy away. Deciding he'd done enough for the day, he headed up to Last Frontier Lodge for some skiing. He skied almost every weekend when there was snow on the ground, so this was typical for him. He felt out of sorts about it due to Ivy's connection to the lodge. He couldn't let that interfere with doing what he loved, so he ignored it.

It didn't take long for skiing to give him exactly the escape he sought. He breathed in the crisp air, scented with fresh snow and spruce, as he flew down one slope after another, pushing himself to exhaustion after a few hours. When he swirled to a stop at the base of the mountain as the light faded to dusk, he was leaning over to step out of his skis when he heard his name. Glancing up, he saw Cam heading his way with a pair of skis in hand. With his cheeks ruddy from the cold and his hair windblown, Cam looked to have been out for most of the afternoon as well.

Cam reached him and paused. "Good ski today?" he asked.

"Always. Snow was perfect, nice and dry."

Cam nodded, his eyes scanning the ski slope behind them. Skiers still dotted the slope and would for hours more. The lights lining the slope came on just then. Cam looked back at Owen. Owen could tell he was considering something, and he couldn't help but wonder what Cam might be thinking. He'd managed to keep his hands to himself last night during dinner with Ivy, no small feat given what her mere presence did to his body. Yet, he wasn't stupid and knew Cam had to sense something, what with Ivy leaving with Owen and not returning last night.

Cam finally spoke. "So, you're seeing Ivy."

Owen finished stepping out of his skis and straightened, gathering the pair of skis together in one hand. He met Cam's eyes, considering how to respond. It wasn't that he was trying to hide anything, it was more that he couldn't quite believe he'd stumbled into this situation. His idea, which was looking more stupid by the day, to give into the raging, burning, yearning that flashed between him and Ivy and let it burn itself out, wasn't working—at all. He'd seriously underestimated the depths of his attraction to her and was swiftly discovering the more he tasted her, the more he wanted. Yet, he couldn't stand here and run circles in his mind right now. Ivy's older brother was asking a simple question.

Owen finally nodded and waited to see what Cam would

say next. Cam was quiet for a few beats, his eyes never straying from Owen. "Okay then. Look, I don't get into Ivy's business much. If anything, that's because I've hardly been around. I have to say this though. Don't mess with her. You seem like a decent guy, and it's obvious she likes you. You'd better not hurt her."

Owen absorbed Cam's comment and nodded. "Look, I didn't expect this to happen. I know how amazing Ivy is. You have my word I'd never do anything to hurt her." As he spoke, Owen's mind started spinning. The truth was, he wouldn't ever purposefully hurt Ivy, yet he'd fumbled this badly. This thing with her was supposed to stay in a compartment of his life, so thoroughly enclosed that he shouldn't even be having this conversation with her brother. He'd let this slide way too far. Problem was, any thought of trying to reel back and withdraw from Ivy was unthinkable. He wanted her too much.

Cam held his gaze, those eyes so similar to Ivy's sharp and assessing. He finally nodded. "Okay then. I'll take you at your word." He started to turn away before pausing and looking back. "Delia bottled a fresh batch of hard cider today. You might want to swing by the restaurant and pick some up before you go. Doesn't last long."

"I just might. Thanks for letting me know."

Owen watched Cam walk away, the packed snow at the base of the slope crunching with his footsteps. He remained where he was for several moments, thoughts of Ivy tumbling through his mind. Part of him was screaming out that he needed to back off and fast. He meant what he'd said to Cam, he would never do anything to hurt Ivy. Yet, he feared he'd set himself up to unintentionally hurt her. Because her heart was warm and inviting, and he knew that maybe she'd thought they could do this thing with some distance but distance wasn't a part of her personality. She was wired differently. He tried to think through how he could get them back onto footing that made sense. Every time he considered that, another part of him screamed. He wanted none of it to stop—not the searing hot sex that scalded him to the core, not the intellectual back and forth and watching her brilliance in action, and not the funny, warm side, like when she'd looked up and grinned at him this morning, slyly pointing out he'd put on his shirt inside out. That's how dazed he'd been after sliding inside her slick channel in the shower. Worst of all, the very thing he'd avoided for so many years was rearing its terrifying head. The idea of anything happening to her struck pure terror in his heart.

He gave his head a hard shake and tried to quell the churning in his gut. He strode quickly onto the sprawling back deck of the lodge and headed inside. He left not much later with several jugs of Delia's amazing cider tucked in the back of his SUV.

CHAPTER 14

*I*vy followed Ginger into Misty Mountain Café. Ginger had insisted Ivy needed to join her for a weekend coffee break with friends. Meanwhile, it was snowing. Again. It had been a full week since she'd last spent the night with Owen, and Ivy was starting to think a little distance might be good. Owen seemed out of sorts and was popping in her office less frequently. She was so *not* accustomed to navigating the waters of relationships, and she didn't even know what to call what they were doing. After several days where he was polite and seemed busy almost every time she encountered him, he'd stopped by her office yesterday. The moment he closed the blinds, she got wet. It was as if he'd been desperate for a fix...of her. And her for him. Then, he'd withdrawn again. She kept telling herself this was what she'd signed on for—a chance to burn the chemistry between them to nothing but ashes. Yet, instead of burning out, every time they connected, the fire flashed hotter and higher.

As she followed Ginger into the line in the coffee shop, she realized she was zoning out. Again. She could compete for the most distracted person in the universe these days. All because of Owen. She glanced around the coffee shop. It felt warm and cozy in here with the scent of baked goods and coffee filling the space. Timber beams crisscrossed the high ceiling in the old Quonset hut with bright wall hangings and artwork adding vibrancy. The café was busy, but once she and Ginger ordered coffee, they managed to snag a table when another group departed. Ivy wrapped her hands around her warm cup and took a sip of the rich brew.

"Ooh, yummy," she said with a smile at Ginger.

Ginger nodded emphatically. "The coffee here is awesome. You should order something to eat too, but let's wait for Delia."

As if conjured by her name, Delia walked through the door and glanced around, giving a small wave when she saw them. Delia Hamilton was the chef and manager at the lodge restaurant and was married to Garrett Hamilton, whom Ivy had met briefly. Garrett was one of Gage's brothers and a partial owner of the ski lodge with the rest of their siblings. When Ivy had first met Garrett, she'd been surprised to learn he was married to Delia. He was a former corporate lawyer and gave off an aura of sharp intellect and persistence. Ivy imagined she'd want to be on his side in the courtroom. Delia with her honey blonde hair, warm blue eyes and soft personality threaded with the steel of being a single mother for years had seemed an odd fit for Garrett. Then, Ivy saw them together. The connection between them burned so brightly, Ivy sometimes felt like she must be interrupting a highly intimate moment, yet that's how they always felt, so she'd gotten used to it.

Ginger chatted with someone who was passing by the table, while Ivy took a moment to scan the view. She wasn't sure she'd ever get accustomed to the fact that everywhere she turned here offered a postcard perfect view. Misty Mountain was close to the bay and offered a clear view of the harbor across the highway. Boats bobbed in the choppy waters. The mountains were obscured by the clouds and the soft snow falling. Ginger had assured Ivy spring would actually arrive in the next month, but she genuinely enjoyed the winter, so she didn't mind the snow. After she'd gotten accepted into her engineering program, she'd missed the mountains and snow of Utah where she'd been raised. California was lovely, but she preferred the contrasts of seasons.

Delia made her way to them and sat down with a sigh. "So good to be here!" She took a long swallow of her coffee and smiled slowly. "You know the best part about being a chef?"

"What?" Ivy and Ginger asked in unison.

"Having someone else serve me," Delia said emphatically. "I love cooking, but I do it so much that it's nice when someone else magically makes coffee for me."

"It's not magic," Ginger said dryly.

Delia laughed softly. "Feels like it. Anyway, what's up?"

"Let's see, work is nuts and I can't wait for spring. Cam promised me he'd build flowerbeds for me this year, so I'm impatient," Ginger said.

"Oh, where are you going to put them?" Delia asked.

"On the bluff side. We get the most sun there."

Delia turned to Ivy. "What about you? Feeling settled in yet?"

Ivy shrugged. "As much as I can. I know Ginger and Cam say they don't mind me being there, but it'll be good when…"

Ginger cut her off. "Would you stop it? We *love* having you here. You can stay as long as you'd like. Cam doesn't say much about it, but I can tell it means a lot to him. I never met your brother, but I know it was really hard on Cam when Eric died and you being there for him meant the world." Ginger's eyes teared up a little when she reached over to squeeze Ivy's hand quickly. "Family means so much to him, so don't you dare feel like you're in the way. I'm beside myself to see how happy it's made him to have you here."

Ivy was startled at Ginger's exclamation, and it must've shown on her face. Delia glanced between them. "It's easy to miss with Ginger because she's usually sarcastic, but she's super loyal, and friends and family are everything to her. So it's great you're here."

Ivy's chest felt a little tight. Her family had been close growing up, but the life of ski competition meant lots of travel for Cam and Eric before Eric died. She'd taken a semester off to be with her parents and Cam in the aftermath, but life and her studies had taken her away again. She was thrilled to be where Cam was. Their parents had been visiting Cam here several times a year, so she knew they'd see them even more now because they wouldn't have to split their time between visits to her and Cam separately.

"It's awesome to be here," Ivy finally replied. "Speaking of Cam, I should be thanking you because it wasn't until he met you that he finally seemed back to himself. Eric's death hit him hard. I mean, they spent years together traveling and skiing. I can't tell you how happy I was when I saw him with you. His old spark came back."

Ginger's emotional exclamation passed when she rolled her eyes. "Fine, fine. It's only because I'm not bowled over by him. He's such a ski god, I always have to make sure he remembers he's human. The gossip when he moved here was awful, all kinds of women drooling over him."

Ivy choked on her coffee and took the napkin Delia handed her to wipe her chin. "I know, right? You should've seen what it was like when he was competing. Obviously, I don't look at him that way, but he had groupies."

Ginger shook her head. "I'll bet."

Delia turned to Ivy. "Speaking of gossip, Owen has sparked plenty of speculation around here. He's all dark and mysterious and almost never shows his face around town. It's a damn miracle he's actually eaten at the lodge restaurant a few times recently."

Ivy couldn't help it and flushed straight through. Ginger snorted a laugh, but didn't say a word. Delia's assessing eyes bounced from Ginger to Ivy. "Well, it's obvious there's something there with you two. I might not have had a chance to sit down and eat when you were there with him, but the man can hardly keep his eyes off of you. What's up?"

Ivy crossed and uncrossed her legs and considered how to reply. Before she had a chance, Ginger spoke up. "It's safe to say they have a *thing* going on. Owen's totally hot for Ivy and her for him. As for where things are going, maybe she'll fill us in."

Ginger's sly gaze swung to Ivy. Ivy took a deep breath and shrugged. "I guess there's a thing, but..."

Ginger cut in again. "Of course there's a thing! You spent the night with him twice. Unless it was with someone else and you didn't tell me about it." She arched a brow.

Delia's shoulders shook with her laughter, while Ivy blushed wildly. "No, I haven't been busy with two men if that's what you're wondering," Ivy finally managed. "As for what's going on, I don't know how to explain it. We, uh... Well, there's something there, so something happened. I don't know where it's going, or what to do now."

Ivy chewed on the inside of her mouth and looked between Delia and Ginger, hoping perhaps they could help her figure out how to interpret the situation. Ginger cocked her head to the side. "Okay, maybe I'm slow here, but you spent the night with him, so I'm guessing something actually happened. You know, like sex?"

Ivy wouldn't have thought it possible, but her face got even hotter. She managed to roll her eyes. "Yes, sex."

Ginger rolled her eyes right back. "Okay, so is this just a sex thing? Or have you talked about something else?"

"That's the thing. We did talk. I don't want complications at work and neither does he, so we figured we'd get each other out of our systems. It doesn't seem to be working though." Ivy heard her words and almost burst out laughing. She sounded so cosmopolitan—as if she'd done something like this before. Maybe that was the problem. She was in so far over her head, she didn't know what to expect. Maybe this deepening intensity, the intimacy that threaded between them, stitching tighter and tighter every time they were together, maybe it would rise and fall before it dissipated.

Delia took a sip of coffee, her gaze thoughtful. "What do you mean it doesn't seem to be working?"

Ivy threw her hands up and let them fall. "Just that. The, the… oh I don't know what to call it!"

"I think you mean raging lust," Ginger added helpfully.

Ivy threw a balled up napkin at her. "Whatever you want to call it. It's not going away. Actually, it's getting worse."

"Define worse," Ginger said with a sly grin.

Delia turned to her. "Stop teasing. You're not going to make her spell out the details here."

Ivy grinned at Delia. "Thanks for the back up."

"No problem. Back to what you were saying, were you looking for advice or support?" Delia asked.

Ivy met Delia's warm blue gaze and pondered her simple question. "Both?"

Delia grinned. "Okay, let's start with advice. Usually I get stressed out when I don't know what to do, especially when it's something to do with relationships."

"Okay, what should I do?"

Ginger's sly manner disappeared. "The first thing to ask yourself is what do you want?"

Ivy sipped her coffee and considered Ginger's question. Before she actually allowed herself to get skin to skin with Owen, she'd have said she merely wanted a chance to actually experience the wild, thrumming desire with him. But that was back when she had no clue. Their chemistry and the resulting connection were like a self-replicating force. Almost like the battery project—every time they tamped down the flame, it fed back into itself, charging and recharging with no end in sight. Aside from the spectacular failure of their silly plan, she hadn't anticipated the growing intimacy she felt with him.

Owen held himself at a distance, yet it was clear he cared deeply about others. He portrayed himself as a man who was driven solely by his passion and belief in creating sustainable energy. The tragic death that spurred him was never mentioned. Whenever she thought about his parents dying, her heart ached. Joan and Derek had given her bits and pieces that fleshed out the man she was coming to know. He was incredibly loyal to the staff who had followed him since he started Off the Grid. He was quiet and reserved, yet his actions were crystal clear. The company's generous pay and health benefits were legendary. Everything about Off the Grid was family friendly, yet Owen had no family to speak of. As much as she didn't know if she had the right to want more from him, it bothered her to see and feel the walls he kept around his heart. As she sat there pondering what she wanted, she realized it might be too late for her to try to make a reasoned choice about this. Owen had slipped right into her heart without even trying.

She gulped her coffee and glanced between Ginger and Delia. "I think I'm in trouble."

* * *

HOURS LATER, Ivy tucked her hands in her coat and stared out over the bay. After she'd come to the startling realization about just how much Owen was coming to mean to her, Ginger and Delia had tried to offer some advice, yet Ivy had merely shaken her head. The glaringly obvious problem was that Owen had made it abundantly clear he wasn't interested in more than whatever it was they were doing. She tried to cling to the burgeoning intimacy between them, but she sensed that very factor might be what was driving him to pull back from her.

After they'd gotten home from coffee, Ivy headed out for a walk on the beach. Ginger and Cam's home was on a bluff overlooking the bay with a winding path down to the beach through trees and a few rocky areas. Ivy gulped in the salty air, savoring the refreshing chill, and wondered what the hell to do now. She sensed it would be an utter disaster to tell Owen anything about how she was feeling. Why, oh why, did she have to go and fall for him? She couldn't help but think she'd have had heaps more sense about the whole thing if she'd ever done anything other than go on a few random dates here and there. She might've recognized the potential contained in the sparks between her and Owen and known to steer clear. Instead, she'd been stupid enough to think she could handle herself without getting hurt—as if she could juggle hot embers in her bare hands.

She resumed walking, her eyes traveling along the beach, which offered a plethora of colorful rocks mixed in with the pebbled gray stones. She paused to pick up a deep red rock, surprised at its lightness. Turning it over in her hands, she guessed it must be a lava rock. She spun to look out over the water again and wondered if Mount Augustine was the source of this small rock. With Alaska situated in the famed Ring of Fire, there were six active volcanoes in the vicinity. Although Mount Augustine was the closest possibility, this small, gorgeous rock could've come from any volcano nearby with the tides sending it rolling through the ocean to land.

She tucked the lava rock in her pocket and continued along the beach. Gulls called, a few eagles flew above and the wind kept gusting. She could smell the hint of spring to come with the air softening the slightest bit. The walk settled her nerves, but she didn't manage to get her mind off of Owen. By the time she turned back, she came to the conclusion she needed to tell Owen they should try to take a break. She had enough sense to know she couldn't snuff out her desire for him, but maybe she could get it to quiet down if they didn't keep fanning the flames.

CHAPTER 15

Owen stalked into his office and slammed the door, the glass rattling slightly. He strode to the windows and stared blindly over the view. His heart was banging inside his chest and he felt sick. Ivy had told him she wanted to talk this morning. He'd been stupid enough to agree, thinking perhaps she wanted to discuss a few details on the battery project. No, instead she'd said she thought maybe they should try to return to keeping things platonic. He could tell she must've practiced what she was going to say because she rushed through it. He'd been too stunned to do anything other than nod. He'd had a conference call lined up right after that and then jumped into a meeting with Derek. He'd barely been able to concentrate. It was so bad, Derek had finally just told him to leave. Derek had enough sense not to give him grief, but Owen had seen the look in his eyes.

His chest was tight and he wanted to storm into her office and demand she reconsider. He wasn't ready for... *For what? You told her this was sex only, a way to get this out of your system. She's respecting that, so why are you so upset? It shouldn't matter. But it fucking does! It's not just sex. It's so much more and you know it. What the hell are you going to do about it?*

Owen kicked the steel beam running through the center of the windows and spun away. He'd completely underestimated this thing with Ivy. He needed to stop calling it a thing. The connection between them had its own force. Sex was only one part of it and everything else fed the fire burning between them—her brilliance, her shared passion for their work, her basic kindness, and her occasionally sly humor. He was in thrall to her and could hardly stand the idea of trying to keep things platonic. Yet, the depth of his feelings for her terrified him at his core. He couldn't stand the idea of letting someone mean so much to him. He didn't know if it was already too late, but perhaps she had a point. Maybe if they let things cool down, the intensity between them would fade.

Another kick to the steel beam and he forced himself to get to work. He'd turn to what helped save him after his parents died—work. He'd pour himself into it and keep his distance from Ivy.

* * *

Ivy was making her way back to the trail that wound up the bluff behind Ginger and Cam's house after another long, chilly walk on the beach. She'd found herself meandering down here with frequency ever since she'd dredged up the nerve to tell Owen she thought they should try to get back to a platonic state. The conversation had been stilted and horrible, and she'd been swinging between regret and relief ever since. Regret because it almost physically pained her to sever the intimate connection between them, and relief because her heart was nearly aching for him and everything she knew she could never have with him.

Long walks early in the morning and before darkness

fell gave her a bracing shock to her system. It didn't help get her mind off of Owen, but then nothing did. Her phone vibrated in her pocket, and she paused to tug it out, answering without bothering to look at the screen.

"Hello?"

"Ah, Ivy. Glad you took my call."

Dr. Parkhurst's nasally voice sent a cold chill down her spine and dread clenching in her gut. She was so startled, she froze for a second, unfortunately giving him a chance to speak again. Once he began speaking, she decided to listen if only to get a sense of what he was after with these calls.

"Look, I'm starting to understand you seem to have genuinely misunderstood my actions. I stayed out of the way because HR told me to. Now that you're no longer employed here, I think it's high time we cleared this up. If you insist on pursuing your formal complaint, I'll have no choice but to sue you for defamation of character. I don't mean to sound threatening, but just as you have a right to protect yourself, so do I. I was hoping we could talk and straighten this out. I've been in touch with Owen Manning, and I'm sure he would appreciate a visit from me to Off the Grid. We could set up a time to meet when I'm there and clear this whole thing up."

Ivy's heart was pounding in a fear-fueled rhythm, and she swallowed against the bile rising in her throat. She'd been so stupid to think she could rid herself of Dr. Parkhurst. She stood there with the cold ocean breeze gusting against her cheeks and couldn't find a word to say. Yet, she knew she couldn't stand to hear his voice anymore, so she hung up on him and quickly went into her phone settings to block his number. She had enough sense to know he'd probably try again from a different number, but she would make sure to check who was calling before answering and not take any calls from unfamiliar numbers.

She remained where she was, looking out over the

water. The snow was gradually receding from the mountains across the bay, the white line marking its end crawling upward day by day. It had snowed again the other day, and Cam warned her to expect a few more late winter and early spring snowstorms, but she could sense spring coming. It was present in the quickening sense of air around her. She took several slow breaths, trying to calm the sick feeling in her stomach and chase the fear away.

She knew Dr. Parkhurst couldn't physically cause her harm anymore. Yet, her instinctive fear wasn't entirely unfounded. Before she'd filed her formal sexual harassment complaint against him, he'd genuinely frightened her a few times by showing up in her office at odd hours and getting far too pushy. He was a large, imposing man. Cornering her once between her office door and a file cabinet had been the last straw. He'd tried to kiss her and refused to move even after she'd asked several times. She'd been pinned by the file cabinet with her face turned away, her back against the wall and him mere inches from her with his meaty hand cupping her cheek. Only an interruption from the janitor knocking on her door had helped her get out of that.

She gave herself a mental shake, her eyes scanning the water. A seal lifted its round head from the water, only a few feet from shore, and eyed her curiously. She'd come to enjoy the antics of the seals and otters she sighted almost daily. Seals tended to follow her when she walked, peeking out of the bay occasionally as if to check where she was. This one held still, its dark brown eyes round and curious as it watched her. "Hey you, I bet you're having a better day than me," she said conversationally, as if the seal could understand her.

The seal kept watching and slowly sank down into the water, its tail flicking as if in goodbye when it swam away. Ivy felt suddenly alone and silly for thinking the seal was keeping her company. She had an abrupt urge to find Owen, to lean into his strength, to lose herself in the heartbeat of passion and intimacy between them. Yet, she couldn't do that, or she'd set herself up for even more hurt.

She spun away from the water and jogged up the trail to the house, her mind spinning over what the hell to do about Dr. Parkhurst. She couldn't help but wonder what Dr. Parkhurst meant when he said he'd been in touch with Owen. She didn't think Owen would've communicated with him in any way, but doubts were crowding her mind right now. When she stepped into the house from the back door off the deck, Cam was coming in through the front door, and Ginger was busy in the kitchen. Cam toed his boots off and looked across the room at Ivy.

"What's wrong?" he asked.

Ivy had been unguarded when she came in, so she figured the jumble of emotions Dr. Parkhurst's call had elicited were showing on her face, chief among them gnawing worry and tension. She looked over at Cam and started to shrug and feign a smile, but it wobbled. He hung his jacket and crossed the room to where she stood. "You look upset. What is it? Did Owen...?

Ivy stalked past him to kick off her boots and hang up her jacket. "It's not Owen! Good grief, since when do you police my love life?"

"Since I know anything about it," Cam replied swiftly.

"Well, you might as well know there's nothing to worry about with Owen. I broke things off, so don't go blaming him," she retorted, fighting the urge to burst into tears.

Cam's eyes widened. Ginger had stopped what she was doing and stood in the archway into the kitchen with a spatula in hand. Cam's far too assessing eyes coasted over Ivy's face. "Okay, more on that later. What's got you so upset?"

Ivy crossed her arms and willed herself to stay calm, although anxiety knotted her chest. "Dr. Parkhurst threatened to sue me for defamation if I don't drop my complaint against him."

Cam's gaze went from puzzled to furious. "What?" His voice was low and cold.

"Just what I said." Ivy dropped her arms and brushed past Cam to the kitchen. "I need a drink. What do we have?"

"Wine, beer or hard cider?" Ginger asked quickly as Ivy stomped past her.

"Wine."

Ivy plunked down at the table, while Ginger quickly poured two glasses of wine and handed Cam a beer.

"Okay, so Dr. Parkhurst is a total asshole, but you already knew that. Don't you dare drop your complaint. You can fight this and win," Ginger said firmly, her blue eyes flashing as she sat down across from Ivy.

Ivy shook her head, emotional weariness taking over. "How? I get decent pay now, but I don't have the resources to fight something like this. Plus, where would I get a lawyer to help? Diamond Creek's amazing, but I'm guessing there aren't tons of attorneys here."

"Maybe not tons, but Garrett Hamilton's about as good as it gets anywhere. He didn't get famous in Seattle when he was doing corporate law for nothing. Guy's a shark, although he's nice as hell. I'm calling him right now," Cam said firmly as he pulled his phone out.

Cam stood up to make the call. For a moment, Ivy wanted to yank the phone from his hand, but the anger faded as quickly as it came. She knew Cam was only trying to help despite her mixed feelings about it. Ivy looked to Ginger. "I can't afford an attorney. I can't do this. I just want this stupid mess with Dr. Parkhurst to end." She took a long swallow of wine and set her wineglass down with a sigh.

Ginger was quiet for a moment and took another sip of wine. "You *can* do this. You already did the hard part. You filed the complaint against him and left the university. My guess is he's just bluffing. Call him on it, and he'll back down."

Cam stepped back into the kitchen. "Garrett said to stop by tomorrow morning. I'll go with you."

"Cam, I can't afford an attorney. I used all my savings to move and I'm not about to..."

"Ivy." Cam leaned against the counter and crossed his arms, his eyes determined and his tone firm. "Garrett won't charge you. You're a friend and he'll take care of it. Don't argue with me about this. I'm not going to stand by and let that asshole bully you. I'm guessing Ginger's right. We'll call his bluff and he'll back down. A call from Garrett will probably be all we need to do."

Ivy stared back at her brother. Cam was pretty low key most of the time, but he had a stubborn side. She sensed if she tried to argue the point, he'd barrel ahead without including her. As tense and emotionally weary as she was, it was such a comfort to have family and friends rallying so quickly to help her. The entire time she'd been fighting off Dr. Parkhurst's advances, she'd kept it to herself all the way to the last few months. She'd been mortified and afraid she was somehow responsible. As such, she'd gone through it mostly alone and constantly worried about her career and how to get him to leave her alone. It was such a relief to have Cam and Ginger's unyielding support. She only knew Garrett in passing, but obviously his friendship with Cam and Ginger was enough for him to offer to help her.

She took another swallow of wine and leaned back in her chair, a tiny bit of tension easing inside. "Okay, okay. I'll go with you to meet Garrett."

Cam let his arms fall, relief evident on his face. "Good." He stepped to Ginger's side and dropped a kiss on the back of her neck. "I need a quick shower. Be back in a few."

After he jogged upstairs, Ginger stood and checked on whatever she'd been cooking on the stove.

"What's for dinner?" Ivy asked.

"Sautéed veggies with a balsamic vinegar glaze, and there's a pork roast in the oven," Ginger replied as she checked the oven and set the timer again. As soon as she sat back down, she pinned her eyes on Ivy. "Okay, what the hell is going on? You told me you really liked Owen. Why the hell did you break things off?"

Ivy took a gulp of wine and fiddled with the salt shaker on the table. "I had to. He made it really clear he just wanted to get me out of his system. He doesn't talk about it much, but it's totally obvious he doesn't do relationships. I don't know what I was thinking to begin with. I was in over my head right out of the gate. It's not even like I broke things off because there wasn't anything to break off."

Ginger drummed her fingers on the table. "Okay, maybe I get why you might think that way, but the vibe I get from Owen is that it's more than sex. That man is seriously into you."

Ivy's heart skipped a beat at Ginger's comment, but the moment of joy was fleeting. Owen's response, or complete lack thereof, to her suggestion they try to cool down had communicated much more than he could've said. His eyes had shuttered, and he'd simply nodded and left her office. Since then, he'd been scrupulously polite and kept his distance. Ivy met Ginger's gaze with a shrug. "It doesn't really matter if he doesn't want to do anything about it."

The oven timer went off, and Ginger stood to check the oven. As she carefully slid the pork roast out of the oven, she looked back at Ivy. "Well, it definitely won't matter if you won't do anything about it either."

CHAPTER 16

Owen was buried so deep in data he didn't even hear his phone ring. A few minutes later, he got up to start another pot of coffee and saw his screen blinking with a message banner from an unfamiliar number. Mildly curious, he tapped play and heard Cam Nash's voice asking him to call when he had a chance. Owen started the coffee and grabbed his phone to hit redial.

"Cam here."

"It's Owen. What's up?" he asked. He couldn't say why, but Cam calling had him worried about Ivy. He tried to recollect if Cam had ever called him and didn't think he had.

"Thanks for getting back so quickly. Look, I'm calling about Ivy. Just to give you a heads up, she's probably going to be pissed I called, but I'll deal with it," Cam said.

Owen's gut clenched. "Is she okay?"

"She's fine. She had a call yesterday from the asshole who chased after her at her last job. He's threatening to sue her for defamation if she doesn't drop her complaint against him. I called Garrett Hamilton about it, and we met with him this morning. Garrett thinks she's got a solid case, and he's willing to take the case at no cost, but Ivy's being stubborn about it. I think she's just tired of the whole mess. Anyway, I'm calling you because she's worried he might try to get to her through you somehow, so I figured I'd better give you a heads up."

Hot anger coiled inside Owen. Gripping the phone tightly with one hand and curling the other in a fist, he paced back and forth in front of the windows. "This is bullshit," he finally said.

"I'm with you there. Just do me a favor and keep tabs on calls that come through for her there," Cam said.

"Anything else I can do to help?"

"Persuade her to let Garrett help out."

"I'll do my best. Mind if I call him myself?"

"Go ahead. I'll warn you though, Ivy's really not too thrilled with this kind of help."

Owen shrugged. He was too angry to care much how Ivy might feel about his interference. He'd be damned if he'd stand by while she let Parkhurst bully her into dropping the complaint. "I'll deal with it. Do me a favor and keep me posted, okay?"

"You got it. You do the same if you hear anything, okay?"

"Of course. Thanks for calling."

As soon as he hung up the phone, Owen strode quickly from his office to Ivy's, his anger barely leashed. Her coat was draped on the armrest of one of the chairs, but she wasn't in there. A quick check on the shared office calendar showed him she was in a scheduled meeting. His anger barely below boiling, he stalked back into his office and poured a cup of coffee. Pacing back and forth in front of his windows, he fought the urge to call Parkhurst and raise hell. The single factor holding him back was the knowledge that Parkhurst would thrive off the attention of a call like that. It would feed the thrill he was getting from threatening Ivy.

In between flashes of anger, Owen wrestled with the unfamiliar desire to protect Ivy. He didn't feel this way about women. He kept his distance and didn't have to worry like this as a result. Yet, Ivy had slipped right through his well-planned defenses. Hell, he'd planned so well to keep this type of emotion out of his life, he hadn't even seen it coming when he met Ivy. He missed her like crazy. Every night, he wished she were there with him. Every day he didn't get a chance to kiss her, even just once, was like walking through a desert with no water in sight. Everything seemed dry, parched and endlessly the same. The bright spots were when he saw her. Those moments were painful too. The desire to touch her, to reinforce their connection, was so acute, he nearly ached inside at holding back. He knew he was coming across as distant and irritable, but he didn't know how else to be and keep a handle on his feelings.

He paused in his pacing to stare out the windows at the view that he relied on to soothe him. Ivy, or rather his unmanageable feelings for her, had unsettled him in ways he'd never expected. Every time he considered whether he could persuade her to knock down the boundary she'd erected between them, he batted the idea back. He couldn't be the man she wanted and most certainly not the man she deserved. He was fixed in the way he was—intimacy wasn't something he could let into his life. The small taste he was experiencing now, the tremors rippling through him at having to keep his distance from her, was nothing like it would be if he let the reins loose on his feelings for her. If anything ever happened to her after he did that, he knew he couldn't take it. It would crush him and that wasn't something he could tolerate again. It had taken many small miracles to drag himself beyond the earth-shattering loss of his parents. The very idea of allowing himself to care that deeply for anyone ever again struck terror in his heart.

He spun away from the windows and took a gulp of coffee. He slipped his phone out of his pocket and looked up Garrett Hamilton's number.

* * *

IVY WAS DISTRACTED as she returned to her office. Blessedly, it wasn't because she was thinking about Dr. Parkhurst's threat to sue her. Rather, she'd just received the latest data from the various test designs out and about, and the results from the one up in Barrow, the design she'd modified, continued to send back the best data. It wasn't where she hoped to eventually get in terms of output recycling back to input, but it was moving in the right direction. She was perusing the rows of numbers as she walked into her office and absentmindedly sat down in one of the chairs by the windows without even bothering to look up. At the sound of someone clearing their throat, she whipped her head up to find Owen seated in the chair across from her. Her cheeks heated immediately and her belly did a slow flip. Beyond the fact he'd startled her, she'd been scrupulously trying to keep from being alone with him. Her body had its own ideas and revved at the mere sight of him. She swallowed and tried to quell her racing pulse.

Her hungry gaze nearly devoured him. His eyes were dark, tension evident in the lines of his face. Even still, he was so damn handsome he took her breath away—literally. His chiseled features, his piercing gaze, his muscled shoulders, well, basically every inch of him—her physical response to him ran so deep, she was wet instantly.

He angled his head to the side, his eyes coasting over her. He didn't say a word, and even though she had no idea what was passing through his mind, it felt like he was eating her up with his eyes. His shoulders rose and fell with a deep breath before he leaned forward, resting his elbows on his knees. He gestured to the papers she'd dropped to the floor in the midst of staring at him like a fool. "Must be interesting."

"Oh right." Flustered, she leaned over, gathered the papers together and set them on the table to the side of her chair. "It's the latest report from the test designs."

"How's the data look?"

Her heart gave her ribs a hard kick. Aside from the fact that he had the ability to melt her on sight, it was just too much that she knew he was genuinely interested in what she might have to say about the data. He'd bat ideas back and forth for hours and listen intently to her feedback. With her heart pounding, she met his gaze and managed to speak. "Good. The modified test design in Barrow is showing the most promising results, and they're fairly consistent even with weather variations. I plan to take some time this weekend to think about ways to tweak the design more to improve the return input."

He nodded firmly. "Good. You're on the right track with that one. I'm confident we'll get it to where we want."

Uncertain what else to say, she nodded and fiddled with her bracelets. His eyes held hers for a long moment before he spoke again. "I, uh, stopped by to let you know I called HR at the university about Parkhurst."

Annoyance flared inside, and she opened her mouth to protest. With Cam barging his way into helping her, it was another level of frustration to have Owen doing the same. He held a hand up. "Hear me out, okay?" She managed to nod and leaned back in her chair, her pulse pounding for more than one reason now. When she was quiet, he continued. "Cam called because he wanted me to screen any calls if Parkhurst tried to reach you here. I'm sure you'll be plenty pissed he called, but it's a damn good thing he did. Parkhurst has already tried to call into your office through the main line today. I alerted Joan, so she made sure office staff don't put any calls direct to your office. He also emailed me again." Owen paused and ran a hand through his hair.

Though part of Ivy was annoyed as hell that Owen had already interfered, another part of her was relieved and comforted to know he cared enough. She couldn't help but feel a sprout of hope unfurl inside, which she promptly stomped down. She couldn't go there with him. Owen was a good man who took care of the people in his life. He would do the same for anyone working at Off the Grid. "What did he email about?" she finally asked, trying to stay focused on the actual conversation, rather than letting her mind wander to all kinds of inappropriate fantasies.

"Said he wanted to discuss coming up to tour Off the Grid, again offered to consult with us on projects and specifically asked about what you're working on. Don't worry, I'm not replying. Trust me, I want to give him hell, but he's not worth the bother and he loves attention. Makes him think he's important. I decided I'd just call HR to share my concerns. Maybe you don't want to, but I'm not going to stand back and let him bully you. Cam mentioned he threatened to sue and he'd set up a meeting with Garrett Hamilton. How'd that go?"

With that nervous dread only Dr. Parkhurst could elicit spinning in her stomach, she fiddled with her bracelets and tried to consider how the meeting with Garrett went. "I guess I should say it went well. Garrett thinks I don't need to worry. He was pretty blunt that Dr. Parkhurst could make things difficult just by filing, but he says as long as I have representation, he can shoot it down quickly. The thing is I can't afford an attorney, and I don't feel right not paying him. I want to deal with this on my own and..."

Owen leaned forward again and shook his head sharply. "Too late. I'm not letting you deal with this on your own and neither is Cam. If you're worried about paying Garrett, you can let me pay him up front and we'll figure it out later." His voice was low and held a hint of warning.

He'd finally pushed too far. Ivy stood up swiftly, anger flashing inside. "No! You're not paying legal fees for me. Why do you care so much? You wanted to keep things simple between us. This is not simple. You don't chat with my brother about what's going on, call my former employer and offer to pay legal fees when you want to keep things simple." She was flushed through with anger and paced back and forth by the table. "This is exactly why I said we had to back off. This is way too personal and that's not your thing. You can't do things like this! I can't... ugh!" She couldn't bring herself to say aloud she'd fallen in love with him and needed him to stay firmly in the category of friend from work who happened to be her boss as well, contract employee details be damned.

She stopped her pacing and leaned her hips against the table, her arms crossed tightly. Hot tears pricked at her eyes. This tangle of her worlds was too much. The mess with Dr. Parkhurst was something she'd thought she'd left firmly in her past. To have him still finding ways to rattle her was beyond infuriating. To have Owen interfere and think it was okay to tell her what she needed to do hit her where it hurt. She'd tried to create some distance between them, and his quick acceptance of it reinforced her choice. He didn't want more, and she needed to learn to be okay with that. He couldn't get this involved in her life without making her wish for more. She was so focused on trying to breathe slowly and get a hold of herself, she didn't hear his approach.

His touch startled her, and her eyes flew up. He curled his hands over her shoulders and slid them down her arms. The warmth and strength of his touch felt so good, it was hard to bear. She couldn't have brushed him away if she tried. He slowly slid her arms apart and stepped to within an inch. Her heart beat wildly, and fire roared through her veins. Inside, she was unraveling—every bit of her resistance went up in smoke. All she wanted was Owen. *Now.*

He lifted a hand, and with a flick, the knot holding her hair back fell loose. He sifted his hand through the loose locks and dusted kisses over her face. When he spoke, his voice was like rough velvet. "I know, I know. It's not simple, and I can't figure out how to make it that way," he whispered.

Butterflies amassed in her belly as she looked up into his eyes, his gaze a stormy sky, emotions flickering like lightning. The look in his eyes and the feel of his arm sliding down her back, pulling her against him, chased away the loneliness, the ache of missing him, and how she felt when they were together. His eyes searched hers, as if he was asking a question. Whatever he saw there must've given him an answer. He fit his mouth over hers in a raw, hot, possessive kiss. In a blink, her body was screaming with need. With their tongues tangling, they plastered themselves together. At the feel of his hard, hot length against her core, she gasped into his mouth. He arched his hips into the cradle of hers, and she cried out at the sharp spike of pleasure. He tore his lips free and stepped back. She felt bereft at the sudden absence of his body against hers.

Owen strode quickly to her door and slammed it shut, locking it and closing the blinds. He was back in front of her in a flash. The air around them was so charged, she felt the vibration to her bones. She wore a bulky sweater over a fitted skirt. She'd kicked off her boots on her way into her office. With his eyes locked to hers and his gaze sending a sweet blaze of heat through her, he hooked a finger under the edge of her sweater and lifted it slowly. The cool air hitting her skin further inflamed her, inside and out. Her nipples were so taut, they ached. He tossed her sweater to the floor. The feel of his gaze was so intimate, it felt as if he was actually touching her.

"You're so damn beautiful," he said, his words low and gruff. He stepped closer and lifted a hand, tracing along the soft skin of her neck, down into the valley between her breasts and curling along the soft underside of her breasts. He cupped both breasts with his hands. Her breath came out in a sob when he started stroking his thumbs back and forth over her nipples.

Restless with need, she slid her hands up under his shirt, a soft, cotton jersey shirt that clung to his muscled chest. His skin was hot to the touch. His breath hissed as she slid one hand up and the other down to curl over his cock. With a muttered curse and a flick, her bra fell open and he dipped his head to swirl his tongue around a nipple, his teeth nipping softly as he drew away.

She was lost in the maelstrom and frantic for more. Her channel throbbed as he turned his attention to her other nipple, while she swiftly unbuttoned his jeans and slipped her hand into his briefs, sighing at the feel of his velvety skin under her touch. With a growl against her skin, he shoved her skirt up and lifted her against him. Her legs curled reflexively around his waist, a soft cry escaping when he adjusted her so the hot, slick core of her felt his cock. She was so close, she almost came just brushing against him.

He leaned back and tangled his hand in her hair, his blue gaze branding her. "I missed you. So damn much," he all but snarled.

Emotion crashed through her. With her legs gripping his hips, his cock hard against her, and his arms wrapped around her tightly, she lifted a hand to cup his stubbled cheek. Tracing his lips with her thumb, she swallowed against the tight feeling in her chest. "I missed you too."

His lips crashed against hers again, and they spun back to where they'd been—caught in a deep, overpowering, drugging kiss, so hot she was aflame inside and out. He adjusted her in his arms and turned, reaching behind her to shove everything out of the way and stretching her out on the table. He slowly eased his lips away from hers and stood. Her hips rested at the edge of the table with her skirt bunched about her hips. The cool air against her thighs sent shivers through her. He slid his palms slowly up her legs, parting her knees as he did. By the time his hands reached the juncture of her thighs, her hips were restless and she was near desperate to feel him inside of her.

He dragged his finger back and forth across the silk between her thighs, wet with her need. After several passes, he shoved the silk out of the way and delved into her folds. With two fingers stroking into her channel, he brought his mouth against her. She cried out, gripping his hair with her hands. She'd thought she was nearly mad with need already, yet he proceeded to notch her need up so high, she didn't know if she could bear it. She was shaking, her hips rocking into his mouth, when he finally swirled his tongue over her clit and sent her flying.

He slowly eased away and smoothed a condom on after fumbling in his pocket. He gripped her hips and pulled them just past the edge of the table. With her body still shuddering from the aftermath of her orgasm, she could barely open her eyes when he spoke.

"Ivy."

When she met his gaze, the air around them went taut, alive with the depth of their connection. In one surge, he seated himself within her, holding still for a moment before he began to move. With a slow rhythm, he brought her to the brink again. Pleasure spun inside of her, coiling tighter and tighter. With every stroke, he sank deeper. She curled her legs around him, pulling him closer. She lost all sense of anything but him. The pounding of his hips against hers, the delicious stretch of his cock inside of her, filling her again and again, and the feel of his eyes on her, holding her in the web of passion binding them together. He dragged a hand down her abdomen and circled his thumb over her clit—and sent her flying again. This time he flew with her, his body going taut before a final surge into her throbbing channel.

Their breath came in loud heaves as he slowly curled forward and feathered kisses on her belly, her breasts, her neck and finally her lips.

CHAPTER 17

Owen walked into Joan's office the following afternoon. He was less irritable than he'd been for over a week. To be specific, since Ivy had politely tried to break things off with him. He almost winced at the thought because he didn't get himself into situations where breaking things off was even a passing consideration. Yesterday in her office, he just couldn't hold back anymore. Even if he tried to convince himself it was nothing more than sex, he wasn't that stupid. Oh, the sex was flat out amazing, but what made it that way was the intense connection that beat as if it had its own heart between them. He hadn't quite figured out what to do about that, but he was relieved beyond relieved she hadn't pushed him away yesterday.

Joan glanced up from her desk, her warm brown eyes wide when she smiled at him. "Hey boss, what's up?"

He rolled his eyes as he sat down in the chair across from her desk. "I might technically be your boss, but I hate when you call me that."

Joan winked and spun her chair to face her computer

again, resuming her rapid fire typing. "Get over it. You started this company, so that makes you the boss."

"Maybe so, but you're like family."

She lifted a shoulder in a shrug. "Whatever. Anyway, what brings you to see me this afternoon?"

"Any more calls from Parkhurst?"

"Just one this morning. He asked for you instead of Ivy. I didn't put him through and took a message."

"What's the message?"

"That he called," Joan said with a sly grin.

Owen had filled her in on the situation, so she'd gone into full protective mama bear mode with Ivy. She was enjoying stringing Parkhurst along with messages. He couldn't help but chuckle. He got furious every time he thought about Parkhurst's threat to sue Ivy, so he certainly didn't mind Joan annoying the hell out of the guy.

She stopped typing and spun her chair to face him again, her grin fading and worry entering her gaze. "It's kinda funny to put him off, but what's Ivy going to do?"

He leaned back in his chair and sighed. That was the problem. He might have temporarily slaked his burning need for Ivy, but they hadn't spoken further about Parkhurst afterwards. If anyone could help him sort out what to do about Ivy and his decidedly disconcerting feelings for her, it would be Joan. As much as he didn't want to go there, he was *that* frazzled about it.

"I wish I knew. She says she can't afford to consider paying Garrett and doesn't feel right accepting free legal services from him. I offered to cover the cost, but she didn't like that idea so much."

Joan picked up a pen on her desk and flipped it back and forth between her fingers. After a moment, she pinned her eyes on him. "What's going on with you and Ivy?"

He shifted his shoulders and met her gaze head on. "Why do you ask?"

Joan rolled her eyes with a soft shake of her head. "Because I know you, and I'm not stupid. I see the way you look at her, and it's obvious she likes you. Things seemed, hmm, okay for a few weeks and then you got all cold and distant, your usual MO, around her. Now, you're all up in her business about this issue with her former boss. Don't get me wrong, I know you'd be happy to help out with anyone who works here, but it seems like you might be going a bit above and beyond on this."

He absorbed her comments and forced himself to stay calm. He wanted to tell her to back the hell off and forget about it, but this was Joan. If there was anyone he leaned on, it was her and by extension, her husband Reggie. He closed his eyes and took a deep breath. When he opened them again, she was still flipping the pen back and forth. "Fine. If I knew how to explain what's going on with Ivy, I would."

"How about you start by telling me what's happened?" Joan was nothing if not persistent.

He lifted his hands in surrender and sighed, his chest knotting with anxiety. "Fine. I like her. A lot. I had this crazy idea it was just some chemistry we needed to burn off. Problem is… it's not burning off and it's not just chemistry. A week or so ago, she said we had to back off. So I did. I hated it and it made me crazy."

Joan's expression was unreadable and then she threw the pen at him. "What the hell is wrong with you?!"

He caught the pen and stared at her. He felt awful. He knew what he was doing wasn't fair, but he didn't know how to stop. "I don't know. I thought…"

"Ivy doesn't deserve some schmuck who just wants to get his rocks off. She deserves far more than that. You happen to be capable of much more than that, but you won't even consider it, so you need to stop now. Let's not even get into the potential HR nightmare we could be facing."

The sinking feeling inside churned wildly in his gut. "She's a contract employee," he said dumbly.

Joan glared at him. "Technicality. Especially with what she's dealing with from her last boss. I can't believe you're dumb enough to allow this to happen." Joan closed her eyes and pinched the bridge of her nose before opening them again. "Owen, you're almost like a son to Reggie and me. I realize mathematically it doesn't work because we're only about a decade older than you, but after your parents died, we just wanted to be there for you. I can't count how many times I've told you I wished you'd find someone. I still wish you would. Ivy's about as perfect as someone could be for you, but you can't do this if you're not going to really let it happen. You can't do something halfway with her."

Joan's dark eyes flashed at him, her protectiveness and anger showing. He knew she was right, but he didn't know what to do. Just thinking about actually saying aloud how he felt about Ivy scared the hell out of him. He'd never considered himself particularly selfish, but when it came to Ivy, he was. He didn't want to give up anything he had with her, yet he knew he didn't deserve her because he couldn't give her all of him.

He looked over at Joan as he considered his words. "Look, give me some time. She means…aw hell, she means a lot to me. Let me figure it out, okay?"

Joan's gaze softened, but only slightly. Joan might have a soft spot for him, but she would hold him accountable. "If you could actually give yourself a chance to love someone, well, I think you might finally get past your parents' death. But don't you dare hurt Ivy. If I get even a hint that you might be dragging this out without ever planning to give her a real shot with you, I'll raise hell."

Owen held her gaze and finally managed a nod. Merely trying to talk about his feelings for Ivy tied him up in knots.

* * *

IVY LIFTED her face into the breeze and gulped in the salty air. It was late afternoon on a Saturday, and she'd hopped in her car and headed to the harbor for a walk along the beach there. She'd been restless all morning and needed something to break up her day. She'd been beating back the urge to go to the office, mostly because she worried she'd encounter Owen there and couldn't trust herself around him. Between mulling over what to do about Dr. Parkhurst and Owen, she was almost perpetually off balance inside. She hated to even think of them in the same second in her brain, but those were the only two functioning trains of thought the last few days.

Cam had informed her last night that he didn't give a damn if she didn't want help from Garrett and invited Garrett and Delia over for dinner. She'd felt cornered and annoyed, although she'd finally caved on accepting Garrett's help. She might not like that she needed legal help, but she'd do just about anything to find a way to get Dr. Parkhurst out of her hair once and for all. Garrett had the green light to start working on pre-empting Dr. Parkhurst's threat to sue. She'd mostly seen Garrett's teasing manner before, yet the minute he started talking law, she didn't wonder about his reputation. He was aggressive and ready to pin Dr. Parkhurst to the wall. With the wheels in motion on that, she was mildly relieved, yet she couldn't seem to shake the dreadful tension the whole mess elicited inside.

Then, there was Owen. She was so annoyed she'd given into him the other afternoon. She hadn't been able to stop herself. She wanted him too much, cared too much. She shied away from the word, but she knew she'd fallen in love with him and she had to find a way to get a handle on her feelings. If she couldn't, she worried she'd have to look for work elsewhere. She loved her job like she'd never loved a job before, but she couldn't stay there if she didn't find a way to push her feelings aside. If she had to leave her job, that meant leaving Diamond Creek, which depressed her terribly. It felt so good to finally be close to her brother again, and she'd quickly grown to love the welcoming circle of friends. There was only one engineering firm in Diamond Creek—it was a small miracle Off the Grid happened to be here to begin with.

She gave herself a shake and resumed walking, idly kicking a round pebble on the sand as she did. This section of the shoreline offered a more open view of the bay than the shore by Ginger and Cam's house. All of Kachemak Bay spilled out into view here with the mountains rising tall on the far side and Mount Augustine standing sentry in the distance. Otter Cove Harbor was tucked into a small cove nearby, the boats rocking quietly in the water, and gulls and eagles stationed along the docks. The walk did help clear her mind, if only because she managed to stop thinking so much. As she made her way back to the parking lot, weaving through the faded sea grass, trampled and torn by the cold winter and snow, she heard her name. Whipping her head up, she saw Owen approaching her on the path.

Her pulse set off at a gallop. Without realizing it, she came to a stop. That's what he did to her. Everything else fell away, the world fading to nothing but them. He stopped in front of her, his cheeks ruddy from the chilled spring air and his eyes bright in the gray light. "I saw your car in the harbor lot, so I thought…" His words ran out and he shrugged. "How are you?" he asked after a pause.

"Okay. I thought it'd be nice to see the beach by the harbor."

"Every beach here is like a postcard," he replied with a wry smile.

She couldn't keep from smiling back because it was

impossible not to when it came to him. "That's one way to put it." She turned to face the bay again, watching as a raven took flight from the harbor sign. She gathered herself and turned back. She could do this. All she had to do was act normal. "You might want to know I decided to let Garrett help me out." She wasn't sure why she offered that detail, but she knew he'd ask. She was still disgruntled inside about accepting help, but she needed it.

Owen's eyes widened and then narrowed as he scanned her face. "What changed your mind?" he finally asked.

"I don't like that I need help, but I do. Garrett's pretty confident he can get Dr. Parkhurst to back off for good. I'd like to put the whole thing behind me, so it seemed silly to keep arguing about it."

"Garrett's aggressive as hell when it comes to legal matters. You couldn't be in better hands. I had a message from the HR Department calling me back yesterday. I was tied up, so I didn't get it until after they closed. I'll follow up Monday."

"You don't have to…"

"I know you don't want my interference, but with Parkhurst trying to contact me about you, it's good for them to know. If you want, I won't call without you. Would that make you feel better about it?"

Slightly surprised, she nodded. A curl of warmth slipped around her heart. It was a small gesture, but it felt so good to know he was trying to respect her need not to have everyone take over. "I'd appreciate that."

They stood in silence together for several beats before Owen spoke again. "Don't suppose I could take you to dinner?"

She was so startled, her mouth dropped open. His lips curled in a slow smile, which did funny things to her insides. "I thought maybe we could try an actual date," he finally said, a flash of uncertainty blinking in his eyes.

Just that tiny moment and her heart clenched, a smile tugging inside. She sensed this wasn't easy for him. If he was going to try, even a little, to make what was happening between them real, then she couldn't say no. She met his eyes and nodded. "Okay. When and where?"

CHAPTER 18

Owen watched Ivy walk away from him, the wind catching her hair and swirling it behind her as she reached her car and climbed in. He had to close his eyes and ball his fists to keep from following her. He wanted to demand she come home with him and wanted to fall asleep beside her. Before he'd seen her car late this afternoon, he'd decided he would try to stop relegating his feelings for her to stolen moments at the office. He didn't quite know what he was doing, but he couldn't compartmentalize her to a corner anymore. Dinner seemed like a normal thing to do under the circumstances. He sensed she was guarded against him, and he wanted to show her he was done trying to hide what was happening between them.

Dinner had been one long, slow tease for him. As was the case every moment he was around her, he'd entirely underestimated the effect she had on him. They'd had dinner at The Boathouse Café, the same place he'd taken her to lunch what felt like eons ago now. With her amber hair glinting under the soft lights and her eyes like fire, he'd had a hard time focusing. After she'd peeled off her jacket, he realized she was wearing another one of those fitted, zippered athletic tops, which should have been completely unsexy. Yet, he could barely keep his eyes away from the shadowed valley between her breasts and couldn't stop thinking about sliding her zipper down. He knew what he'd find there—her perfect breasts hidden behind something silky. If he could have, he would've drenched the silk with his tongue before shoving it out of the way. His mind flashed to the way she'd looked the other afternoon— leaning on her elbows on the table, her nipples taut and her thighs falling open, her folds pink and glistening, so damn tempting.

Yet tonight, she'd been warm, but kept up a wall. He wanted to punch through it, but he sensed that would be pushing too far, too fast. They'd finished dinner and he'd walked her outside where she'd politely thanked him for dinner and walked away quickly. Leaving him rock hard with need. He watched her drive away and stalked to his SUV.

When he entered his home a short while later, it felt empty and bare. He'd never thought much about the fact he was so often alone when he wasn't at work. It had certainly never bothered him. It suddenly hit him that Ivy was the one and only woman he'd ever brought to his home. Right here, right now, he missed her presence so much he ached inside.

He swore to himself and kicked off his boots, striding quickly to the fireplace. After he got a fire started, he settled onto the couch where he usually worked when he was home and pulled up some reports he was working on. Hours later, he woke. His laptop had slid between his hips and the back of the couch, his neck was at an awkward angle, and he had a headache. After making sure he'd saved whatever he'd been working on before he fell asleep, he stood and went to the bathroom. He chased down some ibuprofen with water, set the glass down on the counter and stared in the mirror. He had dark shadows under his eyes. He'd been sleeping poorly for too many days, tossing and turning with thoughts of Ivy constantly spinning through his mind.

He turned away from the mirror and climbed the spiral staircase to his bedroom where he tried to fall asleep, yet again failing miserably because he couldn't turn his brain off. Ivy had taken up residence in his heart and mind and wasn't going anywhere.

* * *

IVY SAT at the round table in Garrett's office and stared down at the paperwork he'd just handed her. Garrett was seated across from her, patiently waiting. She finally looked up, her eyes wide. "You think we should threaten to sue him?"

Garrett nodded firmly. "Sure do. You have a case. I'm not saying you should, but if you want to, I'll be happy to take care of it."

When her eyes widened further, he flashed a grin. "Here's the thing: he's playing hardball, so we have to beat him at his game. I'm good at that, so let me handle it."

"But…"

Garrett angled his head to the side and arched a brow. While he didn't elicit even a tiny zing for her, she could certainly see what Delia saw in him. He was devilishly handsome with his dark hair, his blue eyes and his sly sense of humor. "I'm guessing you want to be nice about it." He shook his head firmly, his eyes sobering. "Nice doesn't work. All we're doing is listing what he's done so far and telling him to back the fuck off. This isn't an actual legal filing. It's a letter of intent, an official way to tell him to go straight to hell and if he tries to sue you, it spells out what we'll do if he does. That's all."

She looked over at Garrett and sighed. "Oh right. We're not actually filing something in court." She set the papers down and nodded. "Send it on. You have a point anyway. Being aggressive like this isn't my thing, it's probably how come it took me so damn long to file the HR complaint against him. How do you think he'll respond?"

Garrett grinned. "Can't wait to find out. I love a good fight, but my guess is he'll back down fast. I'm sending a copy to him and to the HR Department. They won't want any part of a suit being filed against them for negligence in their investigation and in failing to protect you after you filed the harassment complaint."

Ivy leaned back in her chair and shook her head slowly. "I guess it's a really good thing Cam talked me into letting you help out. I'd never have the nerve to send a letter like this. I hoped the formal complaint would get him to leave me alone."

Garrett signed the letter as he replied. "Hate to tell you this, but men like him don't usually back off until they're made to. That's what attorneys like me are for. I've got no problem making this as difficult as possible for him."

He stood from the table and walked to the copier in the corner of the room. He tapped a few buttons and turned back to her. "Consider it sent."

"Huh?"

"Just scanned it and sent it via email. The original will go out snail mail this afternoon. All communication is supposed to go through me, so if you get any calls from Parkhurst or HR, call me immediately."

Ivy stood up, a sense of relief washing through her. Garrett's strong support and confidence in his ability to handle this gave her the first hope in months that she might finally put this behind her. "I can't thank you enough," she said as she tugged her jacket on. "I still feel weird you're doing this for free…"

Garrett waved a hand and shook his head. "Don't even think about it. You're like family. I have plenty of paying work. It's nice to be able to help out when and where I can. Plus, I don't get to handle too many testy cases anymore. I like those," he said with a wink.

Ivy laughed. "Good thing you do. Well, if there's any way for me to return the favor, let me know."

"What comes around goes around. Especially in Diamond Creek," he replied with a chuckle. "You headed up to ski before we lose the last of the snow?"

"Actually, that's where I was going now. Cam tells me we probably only have a few more weeks before it's too slushy to ski on the mountain."

"If you're around the this lodge evening, I'll probably see you then," he said with a wave as she reached the door.

She stepped outside and took a deep breath of the bracing air. As she drove up the winding road to Last Frontier Lodge, she felt lighter than she had in over two years. With Garrett's strong support, along with that of her family and friends, she finally thought she might leave Dr. Parkhurst in the dust. Her mind immediately shifted gears, landing on Owen. After dinner the other evening, it had taken all of her discipline to leave before he had a chance to kiss her. Because one kiss and she was lost to him, adrift in the tide of desire. She needed to keep some semblance of sanity with him. She sensed he was trying to show her he might consider her as something other than a furtive desire he kept tucked away. That meant she couldn't just give in every time they were near each other. Of course, she'd gone home hot and bothered and desperate for release. It had taken another dose of discipline to keep from texting him.

A short while later, she rode the lift up the mountain. The lodge was still booked to capacity and the slopes below her were dotted with the bright colors of ski jackets. She swung her legs and looked out over the view. The mountain peaks in the surrounding area were still snowy, but she could see patches of green breaking through along the lower flanks. Kachemak Bay sparkled under the sun in the distance. A soft breeze coming from that direction blew the subtle scent of the ocean with it. She didn't know if she'd ever get accustomed to such a spectacular view. The lift rounded the top of the mountain, slowing automatically. She skied off and paused to glance around. She'd yet to try all of the slopes here and tended to avoid the more advanced ones. As she skied in a slow circle, she swung around when she heard her name.

Owen was skiing toward her from the chair lift. He pushed his goggles back when he reached her. He wore typical ski gear—sleek fitted leggings and top, both black. She could see every inch of his muscled form. She tried to take a deep breath to slow the dash her pulse had taken, yet as usual, he stole her breath. His eyes matched the sky, and his hair was mussed from the wind. He skied to a stop beside her, his skis mere inches from hers. "Hey there. Didn't know you'd be up here today," he said, a perfectly normal greeting.

She must've stared a few beats too long because he arched a brow. *Talk Ivy. All you have to do is talk.* "Hey. I figured I'd better get some skiing in before we lose all the snow." Flutters spun through her belly, and heat slid through her veins. Meanwhile, all he was doing was standing there. He lifted a ski pole in a wave at Don Peters whom she'd met in passing.

When his eyes met hers again, it was as if electricity charged the air around them. She was hot and cold at once, relieved for the cool breeze up on the mountain. He reached over and curled his hand over hers where it rested on her ski pole. She hadn't tugged her gloves on yet where they hung loosely at the ends of her sleeves. His touch hit her like a bolt, right at her core. She had no idea how long they stood like that when someone else calling her name jolted her out of her heated stupor. She glanced around to see Cam skiing in their direction. Owen didn't move his hand from hers, and she didn't want him to.

Cam came to a sliding stop beside them. "Ginger's waiting for you in the restaurant," he said by way of greeting.

"She is?"

"That's what I said. How long have you been up here?" he asked.

"I've had a few runs. I'll take this last one and meet her there."

She glanced to Owen, uncertain what to say. His hand was still warm over hers, the point of connection sending heat radiating through her with every breath. Owen caught Cam's eyes. "Race you down?" he asked.

Cam flashed a grin. "I'll race anytime you want. You taking the same slope down as Ivy?"

Owen glanced to her. "I don't know. Where were you headed?"

"Probably not where you two might like to go. I'll meet you guys down there. Don't wait on me."

Owen gave her hand a squeeze before pulling it away. Her hand was abruptly cold, and she missed that single point of connection instantly. She quickly pulled on her gloves and tried to collect herself. It was ridiculous how much he affected her. This was nothing more than a casual moment interrupted by her brother. Yet, she was all a twitter inside and didn't want him to ski away. She forced herself to push off on her skis, giving Owen and Cam a little wave. "See you in a few!"

With the icy wind blowing past her, she skied down the slope, enjoying the glide of her skis as she curled through the turns. When she skied into the open area where the slopes joined at the base of the mountain, she saw two skiers barreling toward the bottom and knew it must be Owen and Cam. Snow swirled in a cloud around them as they came to a stop. Ivy grinned when she heard them laughing. She slowed her speed and eased up beside them.

"Who won?"

Cam shrugged. "I think we have to call it a tie."

Owen's grin flashed, sending her belly into a slow flip. "Fair enough."

Before she knew it, Cam had invited Owen to join them for an early dinner at the lodge. It wasn't that she didn't want Owen to join them. The problem was more that she desperately wanted any time she could find with him. Seeing as she was trying to get a handle on her feelings and still uncertain how he'd shifted in his thinking about them, she wasn't so sure it was a brilliant idea to have him around. Yet, she couldn't think of a graceful way out and didn't really want to.

Within minutes, she found herself seated in a booth across from Ginger with Owen beside her. Within seconds, she was suffused with heat, hyperaware of his presence beside her. Her body hummed. While she was busy telling her mind to stop wanting him so much, his hand slid onto her thigh to find hers. When he laced his fingers into hers, she nearly melted right then and there.

CHAPTER 19

"So, do you play baseball?" Ginger asked.

Owen had been distracted most of the night, what with Ivy's warm, soft body beside his, but he managed to turn his attention to Ginger. Her sharp blue gaze met his. "Baseball?" he asked.

"Yes. Baseball," she replied, enunciating the word clearly.

"I haven't played in years, but I played some in school when I was a kid. That's about it," he said, curious about her question.

Cam muffled his laugh with a chug on his beer, while Gage's shoulders were shaking with laughter. Ginger ignored them both. "Perfect. You won't mind if I add you to our team this spring then."

"Team?" he asked dumbly. He knew Ivy's presence had him distracted, but this was so out of left field, he didn't know what Ginger meant.

"Diamond Creek Batters," Ginger said, as if he should know what that was. "It's one of our local teams. I help manage it, and we need more players. It'll be great. You and

Ivy can both play. You'll get to know more people in Diamond Creek, and we'll kick ass."

Ivy's gaze flicked from him to Ginger. "Me? I've never even played baseball."

Ginger shrugged blithely. "It's okay. You can be back up."

Just as Owen was about to protest, Quinn Haynes, whom he'd only met for the first time tonight, spoke up. "This his how Ginger recruits. I got roped in last year and apparently she's already committed me for this year," he said with a grin. "It's actually fun. If I can find the time to fit it in, I'm sure you can." Quinn was one of two doctors in Diamond Creek and married to Lacey, Marley's sister. Owen was rapidly expanding his tiny social circle since Ivy's move to Diamond Creek. He found he didn't mind because it meant he got to spend time with her.

He felt Ivy shrug, her shoulder shifting against his arm. "Okay. As long as you don't expect great things from me."

"I'm in," he added. Ivy's yes cemented his own. Any chance to weave his life closer to hers, he would take.

A while later, Owen walked beside Ivy out to the parking lot. His body was nearly vibrating with need. Hours sitting beside her had set him to humming inside and out. They reached her car, which was parked beside his SUV. She curled her hand around the door handle and looked up at him, her amber eyes catching glints from the lights in the parking lot.

"Well, I should..."

"Don't go." He stepped close to her and threaded his hand in her hair, the silky locks sliding through his fingers. He dipped his head to angle beside hers. "Come home with me," he whispered roughly.

He could feel the subtle tremors rippling through her body and nearly groaned in relief when she nodded, her hair sliding against his cheek. He lifted his head and looked into her eyes, seeing his wild desire reflecting back at him in her gaze. He managed to step back, even though what he wanted to do was lift her high against him and take her right here, right now. With raw need pounding through him, he opened the passenger door to his SUV and helped her in.

As he drove home, relieved spring was on the way and the roads were free of ice and snow, he sped along the winding road through the upper portion of the hillside above Diamond Creek. Though his raw need for her nearly overrode everything, his mind kept circling along one train of thought. He might not have been able to admit it, but he'd taken Joan's pointed warning to heart. He knew it wasn't fair to give into his desire over and over again, but he didn't yet know how to move forward. He knew what he wanted—Ivy in every way, in every part of his life. Life without her felt empty and barren. Yet, every time his mind danced along the edges of what that meant, he shied away. He swatted the thought away, for the thousandth time, and reached over to slide his palm over her thigh.

When they walked into his house a few minutes later, he kicked his boots off and immediately went to the fireplace to start a fire. He turned around to find Ivy standing by a bookshelf, her eyes on a photo on the top shelf. It was the only photo of his parents he displayed anywhere. He had others, but they were tucked away in boxes. His heart gave a throb of pain—the loss was old and the pain was dull, but he suspected it would never disappear.

She turned back to him, and he prayed she wouldn't say anything. She was still for a moment, her eyes scanning his face, before she walked to him. She stopped just in front of him. Though she didn't say a word, her eyes held soft understanding in their depths. With his heart banging hard and fast against his ribs, he couldn't speak. The moment elicited a sense of vulnerability he hadn't experienced in years. Not since his parents' death to be precise.

He closed his eyes because he couldn't bear it but for so long. Her hands uncurled from his and slid up his arms, across his shoulders and up to cup his cheeks.

"Owen," she whispered, her voice as warm as her touch.

He opened his eyes, colliding with her amber gaze. The fear beating like wings in his chest receded. He felt suspended in time, held in this warm, intimate place with her, desire mingling with a depth of emotion that crashed through him with such force he could barely catch his breath.

* * *

IVY CAME AWAKE at the feel of a warm palm sliding along the curve of her hip. She took a deep breath, savoring the feel of waking in Owen's arms. She would *so* not mind feeling like this every day. Owen had sent her flying again and again and again last night. She was starting to hope maybe, just maybe, he was letting down his guard. If he did, maybe she didn't have to keep trying to put walls up around her own heart. Because she didn't know if they would hold. She couldn't seem to turn away from this electric force drumming with its own heartbeat between them.

Owen's palm slid down over her belly, his touch sending hot shivers through her. She rolled in his arms, smiling when she saw him. Because he was usually so tidy, she enjoyed seeing him sleepy with messy hair. She sifted her hand through his jet black hair. "You have bed head," she said with a grin.

His mouth curled at one corner. "So do you."

His hand slipped down her belly, through her curls and into her folds, slick with need. In a flash, he shifted above her, his lips mapping their way down her body, hot kisses dusting over her skin. She was trembling by the time he paused, just above where she wanted his touch the most.

She looked down to find his bright blue gaze waiting for her. She wouldn't have thought it possible to have one look nearly melt her, but he held a unique power over her. Her channel clenched, heat streaking through her. She couldn't look away as he slid a finger inside, another joining it. Quivering with need, she moaned as he stroked into her. She cried out when he dipped his head and brought his mouth against her. Her head fell back as he took her straight to the burning edge—his lips and tongue teased her mercilessly while he drove her wild with his fingers. Just when she felt herself quickening inside, he lifted his mouth and drew his fingers out.

At her protest, he moved swiftly, dropping scorching kisses along her abdomen and over her breasts before settling his weight over her. "I want to feel you come," he whispered roughly. In a flash, he yanked the drawer open in the night table by his bed and rolled a condom on. He held still, the head of his cock resting at her entrance. Her channel was throbbing, desperate to be filled. Opening her eyes, she found his waiting for her again. "Don't make me wait," she managed to choke out.

Held in his blue gaze, she cried out when he seated himself to the hilt. He laced his fingers into hers, gripping tightly as he began to move. She was so close to release, she had to draw deep to hold on. She wanted this to be with him—to let loose only when he did. His eyes darkened as he drove his hips into the cradle of hers. She felt him start to go taut and finally let go, her channel throbbing and clenching around him as hot pleasure rayed through her. He shook against her when he cried out, his forehead falling to hers.

A while later, after they'd showered and dressed, she leaned against the kitchen counter and watched while he slid an omelet onto a plate and handed it to her. "Eat up," he said.

He immediately poured the remaining egg mixture into the pan for another omelet, quickly folding veggies and cheese inside. Within a few minutes, he was seated across from her, sipping coffee and digging into his omelet. The morning was so ordinary, well except for the bone melting sex, and felt so good that she didn't know what to do about it. All she wanted was more of all of it...with Owen.

CHAPTER 20

few days later, Owen walked into his office, his desk phone ringing as he stepped through the door. He strode quickly to the table and answered. "Owen here."

"Ah, glad I caught you. Dr. Parkhurst here. How are you Owen?"

Hot anger rolled through Owen, and he gripped the phone tightly. He fought the urge to throw the phone and promptly tell Parkhurst to go straight to hell. If he was going to play this right, Owen needed to find out why Parkhurst was calling, or rather what he thought he could gain by calling. He yanked the reins on his anger and forced himself to keep his voice calm. He knew Garrett had sent his warning shot via letter, yet Owen was well aware Parkhurst likely didn't know of his knowledge of that and of his full support of Ivy.

He might not be ready to let loose with his anger, but he could get a small bit of satisfaction by toying with Parkhurst. "Excuse me? The name's not ringing a bell for me."

There was a loaded silence, and Owen could practically feel Parkhurst's affront through the phone line. Parkhurst cleared his throat. "Dr. Samuel Parkhurst. We've met at a few conferences."

"Oh right. My apologies," Owen said, injecting just enough obsequiousness into his tone to soothe Parkhurst's ego. "What can I do for you?"

Another long pause from Parkhurst. Owen knew perfectly well Parkhurst would like to assume Owen had read his emails. While he had, he wasn't about to let on because it certainly wasn't for the reasons Parkhurst hoped.

"I'm not sure if you've had a chance to review the emails I sent, but I was hoping to touch base with you about Ms. Nash. I had offered to consult on her projects, but I'm going to have to withdraw my offer."

Owen wanted to throttle Parkhurst and spit his nauseating arrogance right back at him. He forced himself to stay on track. "Can't say I got around to reading your emails. Things stay busy around here. As for consulting on projects with Ms. Nash, that's entirely unnecessary. If you know anything about Off the Grid, you should know that I left United Tech to start the firm. Much as I appreciate the contributions of academia to the field, I have no interest in tying my firm to such arcane guidelines. Furthermore, Ms. Nash is brilliant and certainly not in need of any support. I suppose it works out you've withdrawn your offer since it's unnecessary and unwelcome."

"I certainly didn't mean to offend and had no intention of trying to influence your firm's work. My offer was made out of good faith. Ms. Nash..."

Owen couldn't help himself and cut in. "Has no need for consultation and you must know that. It was your program's loss and my gain that she chose to leave there."

"Perhaps. Either way, I wanted to call to withdraw my apparently unnecessary offer and to give you a warning."

"Oh?"

"Ms. Nash is threatening to sue me if I attempt to defend myself against her baseless harassment complaint against me. I had hoped she would come to her senses, but that doesn't appear to be the case. You might want to reconsider her role at your firm. I'd also like to warn you that if she doesn't drop her complaint, I'll go public. All I have to do is drop a few rumors about her being unsuited for the field and coasting on her looks. Every project that has her name attached to it will be called into question. I'm guessing you'd rather avoid the negative publicity that will bring."

Owen closed his eyes and nearly bit his tongue in half, fighting to keep from telling Parkhurst off. He was ready to spew his fury at Parkhurst, but that would give Parkhurst exactly what he wanted. A huge part of him didn't give a damn about Parkhurst throwing bad publicity his way, but he wasn't stupid. Off the Grid was doing quite well, but the firm was new and he needed a plan for how to respond to Parkhurst. It took all of his discipline not to tell Parkhurst to go straight to hell.

"I see," he finally said. "I suppose we'll have to wait and see what happens." At that, he forced himself to hang up.

He stalked to the windows and started pacing, his anger simmering inside. The last thing he needed to deal with was Parkhurst drawing negative attention to Off the Grid. Much as he'd been happy to leave the academic world behind, he knew Parkhurst could make things sticky with a few of the research contracts they had.

At the sound of a knock on the door, he saw Joan through the glass and waved her in. As soon as she saw his face, she crossed her arms. "What is it?"

He leaned against his worktable and ran a hand through his hair. "Parkhurst is threatening to go public about Ivy and try to drum up bad publicity about Off the Grid if she doesn't drop her complaint."

Joan's eyes flashed. "That asshole!"

"Oh yeah, he's definitely an asshole."

"What are you going to do?" she asked. "You can't let him do this."

Owen rolled his head from side to side. "Hell if I know. I'd never ask Ivy to drop her complaint, but he really can call her work into question if he wants. No matter what a loser I think he is, he has connections and he's been in the field forever. I don't know what the hell to do. I'm damned either way. If I don't tell her about this, he can really screw her over. I can't stomach telling her though and watching her do what would be the most practical thing to do—let it go. She's not the first woman he's done this with, and he deserves a hell of a lot more bullshit than a formal complaint with no teeth." He closed his eyes and shook his head. Upon opening them, he met Joan's angry gaze. "Damn if I know what to do."

* * *

IVY DODGED a puddle on her way into Garrett's office. What passed for spring was arriving in Diamond Creek. Ivy was finding spring here meant mud everywhere. Ginger had informed her this morning there was no such thing as spring, but rather mud season. When she reached the steps of Garrett's office, she looked down at her boots and smiled ruefully. They were covered in mud. She kicked them on the stairs to knock off as much as she could before walking inside. Garrett had called and asked her to stop by this morning.

Garrett was seated at the round table by the windows in his office and gave a wave. He quickly finished a call and gestured for her to join him. "Come on in. Coffee?" he asked, standing to fill a cup from a coffee pot situated on a smaller table nearby.

Ivy shook her head as she slipped into a chair. "No thanks. I've had several cups already today."

He sat back down and took a long swallow of his coffee before setting it down. "I haven't had enough," he said with a grin. "Okay..." His gaze sobered. "I asked you to stop by because I had a reply from Parkhurst's attorney and the HR department. End game is here. Parkhurst's attorney sent a very nice apology letter, excusing the 'misunderstanding' and assuring us there would be no further contact from him."

"Really?" Ivy asked.

Garrett nodded, a grin spreading. "Really. Next good news is the university's attorney assures me they are taking steps to formally respond to your complaint and putting Parkhurst on administrative leave at the moment. They've also advised me to notify them immediately if you hear anything from Parkhurst again."

"But what does that mean? They've essentially been saying the same thing all along. The only difference is they've put him on leave now."

"On the surface it may look the same, but legally he'll be in hot water if he steps outside the lines now. He might be tenured, but he's still required to adhere to university policy. Violating it in the middle of a harassment complaint is a big no-no. Now that we've brought this to the attention of the legal counsel there, any wiggle room he had is gone. My guess is he'd like to keep his pension and benefits, so he'll toe the line. If not, I'll deal with it."

"Wow. One letter from you, and suddenly they seem to be taking my complaint seriously."

"Attorneys take attorneys more seriously. Shouldn't be that way, but it is. I'm guessing it feels anti-climactic, but I really think he'll leave you alone now. It's all about costs and benefits. The costs are too high now."

Ivy leaned back with a sigh. "Thank you so much. You

have no idea how much it means to have legal back up like this."

Garrett grinned again. "No problem. I'll be honest, I was hoping for a bit more of a fight, but the response was so quick, they took that off the table for me. It's what I expected, but I wouldn't have minded making Parkhurst squirm a little more."

Ivy started to laugh and next thing she knew, she was laughing so hard, she lost her breath. She finally managed to stop and looked over to find Garrett shaking his head. "Big relief, huh?" he asked.

She took a slow breath, the knot of tension in her chest easing. "Definitely. Well, is that it?"

"For now. If you hear anything from Parkhurst, let me know immediately. Otherwise, consider this a finished matter."

Ivy stood up and slung her purse over her shoulder. "I still feel funny having you take care of this at no charge. If you'll send me a..."

Garrett stood with her, shaking his head firmly as he did. "There will be no bill. Cam's a good friend, and now you are too."

"Okay, okay. Well, thank you again."

He walked beside her to the door, giving her shoulder a squeeze as she stepped out into the bright sunshine. She gave a wave and walked down the stairs. She heard the door close behind her and paused to turn to the bay. A brisk breeze gusted off the water, and she savored the fresh, clean air as she breathed it in. The sun struck sparks on the surface of the water. She turned away, feeling lighter inside than she had in years, since before Parkhurst first started creeping her out when she was a doctoral student. She spun away and started to jog to her car, promptly splashing in a puddle.

A short drive later, she parked her car at Off the Grid

and walked inside. She recalled the afternoon she'd come here for her interview. Her nerves had gone from unsettled to wild the second she'd laid eyes on Owen. As it had been that day, the reception area was quiet. She glanced around and realized she'd come a long way since that afternoon. She'd moved here, started her job and loved it. She couldn't say precisely why, but Garrett's help cemented the feeling that she was actually starting to belong here in Diamond Creek.

The door to the waiting area opened and Joan stepped through with several files in her hands. She smiled, but it didn't quite reach her eyes. "How'd the meeting with Garrett go?"

Ivy had seen her on the way out and mentioned where she was headed. "Great actually. The university put Dr. Parkhurst on administrative leave, and Garrett received a letter from them requesting we notify them if Dr. Parkhurst tries to contact me again. He also got a letter of apology from Dr. Parkhurst's attorney. All in all, it doesn't feel major, but Garrett says the costs are too high now for Dr. Parkhurst to keep bothering me."

Ivy couldn't say why, but the look on Joan's face cued her something was off. "What's up?"

Joan sighed. "You need to talk to Owen."

Ivy's stomach started churning, and she had no idea why. "Can you give me an idea of what's going on? Is it something to do with Parkhurst?'

Joan held her gaze and nodded slowly. "Just talk to Owen."

Ivy nearly ran past Joan. "On my way right now."

She raced down the hallway to Owen's office and entered without bothering to open the door. "What's going on? Joan said I needed to talk to you."

Owen spun around. She didn't know how to read his expression. He didn't say a word and simply gestured to the computer screen in front of him. The relief she'd felt in Garrett's office had turned into a dread filled churning inside. She stepped to the table and looked at the computer screen. Owen had the website for one of the premier engineering publications on the screen. The moment she started reading, she felt sick. The headline read: *Ivy Nash, acclaimed engineer accused of falsifying complaint about famed leader in the field*. She couldn't stop herself from reading further. Dr. Parkhurst hadn't violated anything with HR, but he'd done worse. The article went on to question her doctoral research and speculated she'd only succeeded in the field by coasting on her looks and relying on the expertise of Dr. Parkhurst and others. The article went so far as to mention Off the Grid and speculate as to whether the firm would choose to keep her, knowing her work might not be all it claimed to be.

Ivy's eyes were hot with tears, and she wanted to scream. She looked to Owen, gesturing to the screen. "I can't... this is horrible. It doesn't even matter what I do."

Owen started to stand from his stool, but she couldn't bear it. She bolted, taking off at a run down the hallway and out of the building.

CHAPTER 21

It was dark outside the windows of Owen's office, the stars peeking out between the wispy clouds drifting across the night sky. It was going on midnight, and he was still working. Well, working might not be the best way to describe what he was doing. Ever since Ivy had run out of his office yesterday, he'd set a record for being distracted. She wasn't returning his calls and had sent Joan an email with her intent to resign. He'd forgotten to turn in the completed diagrams on one of the wind turbine projects to the assembly team. As such, the team had wasted an entire day working off of draft designs. Derek had caught the major oversight and corrected it without bothering to check with Owen. He'd yet to speak to Owen about it since. Meanwhile, Owen was so irritable, he'd mostly holed himself up in his office and was ignoring everyone.

He didn't have a clue how to fix things for Ivy with Parkhurst making good on his threat to publicly drag her down. The door to his office opened, the sound alerting him. He spun in his chair to find Derek walking in. Annoyance flared, but he shoved it away. "What's up? Didn't know you were working this late," he said.

Derek walked across the room and sat down opposite Owen at the table. He leaned on his elbows and steepled his fingers under his chin. He looked over at Owen, his eyes assessing.

"What?" Owen finally asked, needled by Derek's long silence.

"You need to pull yourself together and fast. You're like a black cloud around here. What the hell is going on?"

Owen stared at Derek and swore under his breath. He closed his eyes and tried to quell the feeling of dread that had been knotted in his chest. Opening them again, he met Derek's angry gaze and ran a hand through his hair. "This bullshit Parkhurst pulled about Ivy has me all screwed up. She won't talk to me and she sent a resignation letter to Joan."

Derek's perceptive gaze remained trained on Owen. "Do something about it," he said flatly.

"You think I haven't been spinning my wheels on that since yesterday! She'll get pissed if I do anything without talking to her about it and she won't talk to me."

"Do something about it," Derek countered again.

Owen stared at him, his heart getting that funny feeling he didn't like, the one where he felt anxious, uncertain and utterly terrified of losing Ivy. He couldn't quite figure out what Parkhurst's bullshit move had to do with this, but…

When he didn't say anything, Derek leaned back and crossed his arms. "You're scared and you're on your way to doing something stupid."

"On my way?" Owen finally managed to ask.

Derek rolled his eyes. "Sweet Jesus. You are so out of your depth here. I don't have all the details because it's not like you filled me in, but it's obvious you like Ivy. A. Lot. It's obvious she likes you. Difference between you two is that woman wears her heart on her sleeve. For crying out loud, she bought brownies in for Eleanor's daughter to sell at the school bake sale after she overheard Eleanor mention her oven was on the fritz. She does crazy sweet things like that all the time around here. Meanwhile, you keep your distance. You're a good guy, don't get me wrong, but warm and fuzzy isn't your thing."

Derek opened his mouth to continue, but Owen cut in. "Still not telling me what I'm on my way to."

Derek shook his head again. "Impatient much? Geez, dude. I was giving a little context. Anyway, Ivy is warm and fuzzy. Your whole keep your distance, all business thing won't work if you love her. I think you can't find your way out of this stupid paper bag Parkhurst stuffed you in because you're afraid. Fuck him. Make a public statement about what you know and get her back publicly. Big time. We can swat his crap away like the fly it is, but not if you sit on your hands like you are now. If you ask me, you're being a coward."

Owen's heart seemed to be stuck on this endless loop of nearly breaking a rib every few minutes. It gave a swift kick just now, and he closed his eyes to try to slow his pulse. He felt like he was going to burn a hole in his brain. He stared at Derek, his heart giving his practically bruised ribs another kick. "I'm not..."

In a flash, his anger ignited. He couldn't believe Derek had just called him a coward. As quickly as the anger flared, it deflated. He leaned back and ran a hand through his hair. His throat was tight, and he almost wanted to cry. He wasn't the kind of man to say men shouldn't cry, yet he hadn't cried in years. In fact, he hadn't cried since the brutal weeks after his parents died. He closed his eyes and tried to breathe slowly enough that his heart would stop pounding and the pain pressing inside his chest and throat would ease. But it didn't. The word love was something he'd avoided like the plague for years, yet everything Derek said hit him so hard, he knew it was true.

Derek held his gaze, his eyes hard. "Get off your ass and make this right.

That funny feeling Owen didn't like nearly went wild inside his heart. He stared at Derek, feeling sick inside. He finally nodded slowly. His mouth dry, he grabbed the glass of water on the table and gulped it down. "Okay, okay. I'll figure this out."

CHAPTER 22

Owen looked over at Garrett and nodded. "Done. I'll take care of it. You just do your thing and get my back. Actually, don't give a damn about my back, it's Ivy's I'm worried about."

Garrett returned his nod. "Got it. I've got the filing ready to go."

Owen stood from the table in Garrett's office. "Call me when it's done."

At that, he left Garrett's office quickly and zoomed up the hill to Off the Grid. When he walked by Ivy's empty office, which had been empty for days now, his heart gave his ribs a hard kick. Ever since Derek had stopped in the other night, Owen had gone into planning mode. He didn't like acknowledging that he'd frozen on this Parkhurst mess all because he was afraid of his feelings for Ivy, but Derek had been right. Owen was never one to back down from a fight, or give a damn about the kind of bullshit Parkhurst had pulled. He'd called Garrett late that night and asked him to sue Parkhurst for defamation. Owen was teed up to send out a public announcement with the whole sordid story

193

about what Parkhurst had put Ivy through. It had taken three long days to get everything lined up because he was determined to do it right. He'd drawn upon his connections and tracked down three former doctoral students who were willing to go public about their own experiences with Parkhurst.

He slammed his office door shut behind him and sat down at his computer, pulling up the statement he'd written. He'd had Garrett review it beforehand, just to make sure he didn't put Ivy in any legal jeopardy by what he was about to do. He pulled it up and attached it to the email going out to every major engineering publication in the country, along with the chair of every department of any consequence. He hit send and immediately left, determined to find Ivy.

* * *

Ivy stared at her email, reading it again. Her heart was pounding so hard it hurt.

"What is it?" Ginger asked.

Ivy was sitting on the couch at Ginger and Cam's house, pretty much where she'd been camped for days. She was sick over what Dr. Parkhurst had done. She'd turned in her resignation to Joan and ignored every call from Owen. She had to back away because she wasn't going to let her presence taint the good reputation Off the Grid had. Owen couldn't fix any of this, so she needed to make a clean break. She'd also come to the conclusion this gave her a way to back out of the emotional tangle she was in with Owen.

When it came to him, she'd screwed up royally. She should never, ever have thought she could somehow get Owen out of her system and keep her heart tucked away. She didn't fault herself for wanting to, dear god, the attraction between them was enough to set a room on fire. Yet, she was annoyed because she might not have had too much experience with relationships, but she had known she didn't tend to go the casual route. If she had been more of a casual type dater, she'd have lost her virginity long ago. It had been so naïve to stumble into this fling with Owen.

She'd been so focused on getting past the entire mess, she didn't even know how to react right now. She was stunned. She'd just received an email from a reporter asking about her response to the lawsuit filed by Owen against Dr. Parkhurst. Her phone had been blowing up for the last half hour, but she'd ignored every call because she hadn't recognized any of the numbers. She'd finally opened her email to find her inbox filled with inquiries. It wasn't as if the engineering field was all too trendy, but Owen and his work were. She lifted her gaze and looked at Ginger.

"Owen filed a lawsuit against Dr. Parkhurst for defamation of character against me. I didn't know he could do that, but I guess since I was working at Off the Grid…"

Ginger grabbed Ivy's phone from her. "Give me that." She quickly scrolled through the email and lifted her fist in triumph. "Yes!"

Ivy's heart was beating wildly. She didn't even know what to feel, although she couldn't help but feel incredibly pleased Owen had gone to bat for her like this. No matter what, he'd just thrown his own reputation and that of Off the Grid in with her. "Is this good? Isn't it going to make things even messier?"

Ginger handed Ivy's phone back to her. "It's already a mess for you. Owen's just gone big, and I mean *big*, on showing you he has your back. If you wondered whether he loved you, no need to worry anymore. Get your ass off that couch and go see him. I know you've been avoiding his calls like the plague."

Ivy stared at her for a long moment before leaping up.

Hours later, Ivy walked quickly down the hallway at Off

the Grid, passing her darkened office, and straight into Owen's office. She'd spent the afternoon and evening looking for him. She'd tried calling and gotten no answer for hours. This was her third stop by the office after failing to find him earlier. Joan had discovered he'd forgotten his phone here, so that left Ivy running around blindly most of the afternoon.

As she stepped through the door, Owen turned from where he was sitting at the table and her heart gave a little kick. Across the room, the current between them flickered to life, its heat scoring her straight through. She closed the door behind her. It just now occurred to her he didn't have blinds on his office door like she did. Of all the things she'd have wondered she might regret, the lack of blinds on an office door wasn't one of them. Yet, right here, right now, it pained her. She looked over at his bright blue gaze, his rumpled black hair, and his to-die-for body and wished she could slake her instant lust for him immediately.

With a deep breath, she managed to walk normally across the room and stop in front of him, far enough away she could keep her hands to herself. Before she had a chance to speak, he did. "Joan told me to stay put when I got back here a few minutes ago. I've been looking all over for you." His gaze held hers.

Emotion pounded through her. She was still so stunned at what he'd done for her, she didn't quite know what to say. She turned to lean against the table and curled her hands over the edge.

Owen's eyes scanned over her. "I hope you don't mind…"

"Of course not! I can't believe you sued him, and I'm afraid it's going to make things messy for you."

Owen grinned, a devilish glint in his eyes. "Maybe so, but I don't give a damn." His gaze sobered quickly and he stood, stepping in front of her and sliding his hands down her arms to pull hers free from where they were curled on the table and into his. "It's funny, but not really. I'd like to kick his ass for what he put you through."

Her pulse resumed its wild rhythm as she looked up into his eyes. It was getting harder and harder to keep her hope leashed. Her heart was all in when it came to Owen, and he seemed to be trying to let go of some of the rigid walls he kept around his. The air around them buzzed to life, the current that had gone idle for a few minutes revving up.

What she said next startled her. It came straight from her heart, skipping her head altogether. "I think I love you."

The second the words came out, she gasped. His hands tightened over hers. He was silent, his eyes searching her face. With her heart beating so hard and fast, it was a miracle she didn't topple over from the exertion, she stared back, wishing upon wish she'd had enough sense to keep her mouth shut. She hadn't been ready to say those words, the feeling had just welled up and blurted itself out.

When he stayed quiet, she gathered the remnants of her courage and spoke again. "I didn't mean to say that right now. It just, well, it just came out. Don't..."

He stared at her for several beats. His shoulders rose and fell with his heaving breath. Her pulse lunged and her heart clenched. She wasn't certain how to read his expression because all she could think was that he looked scared. Yet, Owen wasn't a man to be scared. He was remarkably controlled. The only times she'd seen him lose his iron grip on control was when they were twined together, their hearts and bodies almost as one. After the quiet dragged on, she couldn't help but reach her hand out. It lifted on its own accord, reaching to smooth her fingertip along his brow and down his cheek, rough with stubble. He hadn't shaved in days, but because he was ridiculously handsome, it only added to his charm. "Owen, are you okay?"

He reached up, his hand curling over hers and holding it fast within his grip. "I'm more than okay."

Her stomach did a slow flip, while her heart beat wildly in her chest.

His eyes were locked to hers, his gaze so intense she had to hold still and force herself not to look away. "I..." His breath drew in sharply, and he closed his eyes. On the heels of another breath, he met her gaze again. "I, uh, I love you. I don't know what I'm doing. I'm sorry I was such an ass and it took me so long to figure it out. I've been trying to call you since the other day and..."

She blinked against the tears pressing at the back of her eyes, one drop sliding down her cheek. "You weren't an ass. My God, what you just did for me is huge." Emotion was rolling through her, yet she couldn't even think, much less believe she could let herself hope simply because Owen said he loved her.

"Oh no. I was definitely an ass and selfish as hell. I wanted to have it all without putting myself on the line. I froze after Parkhurst pulled his bullshit move. Derek called me out, and I realized I was sitting on my damn hands over it because I was afraid of how much you mean to me. When you wouldn't take my calls, I decided I'd do what I could to make it right. I don't give a damn about the negative publicity, but I wanted to do it right, so Parkhurst would get the public beating he deserves."

Another tear rolled down her cheek. "I can't believe what you did. You tracked down those other women and actually filed a lawsuit. Are you sure this won't make things hard for Off the Grid?"

He angled his head to the side and lifted a hand, wiping the dampness off her cheek with his thumb. "I don't care if it does, but I don't think it will. Garrett's on it, so we're in good hands. All I care about is you. Even if you don't stay here, you're an amazing engineer, and you deserve the accolades you've gotten. I want you to be able to rise above the crap he's trying to spew. You will. I know it."

His shoulders rose and fell with another breath. "Enough talking about Parkhurst. Let Garrett do his job." He stepped closer, reaching for her other hand. "I won't pretend I know what the hell I'm doing because I definitely don't. But I love you and I can't stand the idea of not seeing you every day. Please tell me you'll withdraw your resignation and come back. I'll support whatever you want to do, but I love knowing you're right here with me."

Ivy's heart flew skyward, beating hard and fast with pure joy. She yanked her hands free and flung her arms around him, burying her face in his neck. He held her tight against him, one hand sliding up her back in a heated pass and the other stroking through her hair.

When she leaned back to look at him, that dark look had faded from his eyes. Nothing but pure blue, glittering with warmth, shone back at her. "Does this mean…?"

"That I'm sorry it took me so damn long to figure out how much I love you? Yes," he said with a low chuckle. His eyes sobered. She shimmied down and curled her hands around his again. "I don't know if I need to explain why I was so slow about this, but after my parents died, I decided I didn't want to hurt like that ever again. I was stupid enough to think I could control that kind of thing. I just hadn't been tested yet. Then I met you."

"You don't have to explain."

"I need to for me. When I started to understand how much you meant, I didn't handle it well. I thought I could have it both ways. That I could somehow have you without putting myself on the line. That wasn't fair to you. This whole Parkhurst thing blew up, and I didn't know what the hell to do. I suppose the one good thing he did was make me figure out how much you mean to me."

She wouldn't have thought it possible to love him more,

but she did. He was so intrinsically good, so fair and so true. She squeezed his hands. "We both stumbled into this."

His mouth curled at one corner. "That's one way to put it."

With one step, he was so close, she could feel the heat of him. The air shimmered to life around them. She placed her hand on his chest, his heart beating under her palm. He dipped his head and caught her lips in a kiss.

EPILOGUE

*I*vy's footsteps echoed as she walked down the hallway at Off the Grid. She smiled as she looked through the windows comprising the outer wall of the hallway. Snow was falling softly outside, adding to the already considerable snowpack on the mountains. Every so often when she was walking down this hallway, she thought of the day of her interview roughly a year ago now. She'd been so distracted, she hadn't really been able to enjoy the spectacular view unless she was counting the view of Owen. Smiling to herself, she entered her office, tossed her jacket on a chair and immediately powered up her computer.

She loved her job and still occasionally had to pinch herself. She'd ended up with the job of a lifetime and gotten lucky enough to find Owen. With a mental shake, she forced her attention to work. In the past year, they'd made massive improvements on the efficiency metrics for the battery project, but she was waiting on the latest data that would reflect progress from a major design tweak she'd made. She'd sworn the entire team to secrecy and made Derek promise not to breathe a word to Owen. Derek had laughingly agreed. With Owen tied up on the wind turbine projects and having entirely handed the reins to her for the battery project, she'd succeeded in keeping this latest update off of his radar.

She logged into the online monitoring system and pulled up the most recent data report. She scanned it quickly, squealing when she saw the results. She stood so quickly, her wheeled chair rolled back and bumped into the wall. She started to run to Owen's office, but forced herself to stop. She wanted him to see the data himself because that's how he was. Sitting back down, she saved the report and quickly emailed him, titling the email *Urgent: Read Immediately.*

She knew he was in his office because he had an early morning conference call, the only reason they hadn't come to work together this morning. She waited impatiently, eventually forcing herself to work on something else when he didn't respond to her email or show up in her office. It was close to lunch when she looked to the wall separating her office from his and glared at it. "You'd better be damn busy," she said to the wall.

A sound at her door drew her attention. She spun in her chair and saw Owen standing there, his mouth hitching up at one corner. She kept thinking she'd get used to seeing him every day, but not so. Her eyes devoured him—he wore a pair of faded jeans, so soft they hugged his muscled thighs, topped with a navy t-shirt, which brought out the blue of his to-die-for eyes. His jet-black locks were rumpled. Her belly did a slow somersault, her pulse took off on a wild run, and heat rolled through her in a wave. Her need for him seemed endless. Every time it was slaked, it rose again with fervor. He'd already left her nearly boneless this morning in the shower when he slid a hand down her spine and bent her over, sinking into her wet, clenching channel from behind. Yet now, all he had to do was appear, one of his slow, sexy smiles spreading across his face, and she was nearly panting.

He stepped into her office and shut the door behind him. The click of the lock made her squeeze her knees together. When he closed the blinds, she thought she might melt right where she was. He walked to the table and leaned his hands on it, his blue gaze locked on her.

"96 percent, huh?" he asked.

She grinned. "That's right. 96 percent efficiency. Pretty good, huh?"

"Very good. How'd you manage to keep this off my radar?"

"Swore everyone to secrecy. Even Derek."

His low chuckle sent a shiver up her spine. "Damn. I'm impressed. You know how much it turns me on that data gets you so excited."

She flushed and nodded as he straightened and rounded the corner of the table. Without a word, he leaned over and lifted her into his arms, taking a few steps to the chairs by the windows and sitting down with her in his lap. Her legs dangled to one side on his knees. She glanced up, her breath catching at the look in his eyes. His gaze was intent and somber. She lifted a hand and trailed her fingers along his jaw.

His shifted his hips and reached down to pull something out of his pocket. She was puzzled when he handed her a slightly rumpled piece of paper. "What's this?" she asked.

"Take a look."

She unfolded the paper and scanned it quickly. It took her a moment for the details to sink in. When they did, her heart started pounding hard and fast. "Am I reading this right? This says you've already filed to share full ownership of Off the Grid with me."

He nodded, his gaze solemn. "That would be right."

"Owen, you didn't have to..."

"I know I didn't have to do anything, but I tried to think of how I could show you how important you are to me. It may seem weird, but I know how important your work is to you. I wanted to make sure you knew that this place isn't just mine. You're as much a part of it as I am." His cheeks flushed and his shoulders rose and fell with a deep breath. "I hope it makes sense. I just wanted to find a way to show you that I wanted every part of my life tangled up with yours, so..."

She threw her arms around his shoulders, tucking her head against his shoulder. Her mind spun back over the past year. After Owen's lawsuit against Dr. Parkhurst, Parkhurst had settled with a whimper and a public retraction of his prior statements about Ivy. After she and Owen had gotten to the other side of fumbling through the start of their relationship, they'd continued to stumble here and there, mostly because neither one of them had much experience with falling in love. She'd had her struggles to let their relationship be known around the office. She hadn't wanted anyone to think she received special treatment and worried about how the rest of the staff would react.

Both of them had struggled with navigating the tricky territory of being open about their feelings. She'd initially resisted moving in with him, though he'd asked over and over. When Ginger had finally pointed out that Ivy was all but living there anyway, she'd stopped fighting. She'd come to discover she had a rather independent streak and had occasionally floated the idea that perhaps it would be better if she branched out on her own for work. Not many people would understand, but engineering was her first love. Owen was one of the few who met her at that level and could share her passion and joy with the same fervor. Within that context, his gesture was enormous.

She lifted her head and met his eyes, her own tearing up. "I never would have asked you to do this, but I can't even say how much it means because this place is you, it's your life."

He brushed her hair away from her face, tucking a loose lock behind her ear, his touch sending a hot shiver through her. "You mean more. I wanted to make sure you knew that. You're stuck with me now because this is a done deal."

He shifted his hips and fumbled in another pocket, this time lifting his hand and dropping a ring in hers. It was warm from the heat of his body, a simple silver band. Her eyes flew up, hot tears pricking at the back. "Is this...?"

He nodded to the ring. "Read it."

She leaned back. With her hands between them, she turned the ring over in her palm and angled it so she could read the engraving. It read: 2 (2x-i) > 4x-6u. She quickly ran the equation in her mind with the result: i <3 u. She burst out laughing. Leave it to Owen to find a way to use math to tell her he loved her. If she typed the answer to the equation into her phone, it would turn into the emoticon 'i heart you.'

She looked up at him again, smiling through her tears. "So, does this mean...?"

"It means I love you and even though I'm not the most traditional guy, I'm asking you to marry me," he said, his gaze strong and steady.

She threw her arms around him again, savoring the feel of his arms coming around her and holding her close. With the feel of his heart beating in tune with hers, she leaned back. "I think I forgot to say yes."

* * *

OWEN CLIMBED out of his car and took a moment to enjoy the view. It was Valentine's Day, which meant they were deep in the snowiest, coldest part of winter in Alaska. A snowstorm had blown through last night, dumping another foot or more of snow on the mountains. That meant good skiing this weekend. The surface of the bay was choppy this late afternoon with the sky clear and the wind up. White-caps dotted the water, along with a few fishing vessels. The mountains rose high on the far side, strikingly beautiful with their snow-capped peaks. He took a deep breath, savoring the icy air, before turning to walk inside.

He spent a lot more time at home ever since Ivy had moved in. They often worked together when they were home, but working from home with Ivy meant her legs were draped over his lap on the couch while they tossed ideas back and forth, or worked quietly. He'd been obsessing about what to do for Valentine's Day and finally decided he would cook dinner. Ivy had told him way back when she wasn't much of a cook, and he'd found that to be true. She loved it when he cooked though. He'd begun to cook with greater frequency, mostly because he had someone to share it with. He stepped inside and his eyes started watering.

Smoke was billowing from the stove, and Ivy was running around waving a towel in the air. She swung to the door, her hand flying to her mouth. "I caught a pan on fire," she said.

He toed his boots off and walked to the kitchen counter, setting down the groceries he'd carried in. "I didn't know you were planning to cook."

Ivy opened a few windows nearby, chattering as she did. "I wanted to surprise you for Valentine's Day. Delia gave me her recipe for that glazed salmon you like so much, but I burned the glaze."

His heart gave a little kick. With the windows open, the smoke started to clear. Ivy turned to face him, a rueful smile on her face. "So much for an amazing surprise dinner," she said with a shrug.

All he had to do was look at her and he was lost. Her hair was falling loose from its knot, tendrils escaping every which way. Her eyes were like amber fire—always. He loved her so damn much. She was brilliant, kind, funny, beautiful and showed him every day in so many ways how much she loved him. A burned dinner was just one more thing she did perfectly. He took a breath and closed the distance between them. "Good thing I was planning to cook dinner."

She cocked her head to the side, lifting a hand to brush a loose lock of hair out of her eyes. "You were?"

He slid his arms around her waist, nodding as he did. "Uh huh." He couldn't resist and dipped his head to the soft curve of her neck, dusting kisses along her throat.

When he lifted his head again, she bit her lip. "I think maybe I should try a different surprise."

"You still haven't beat your 96 percent surprise,' he said with a chuckle.

Her wide grin was so satisfying, he felt like a fool. He felt like a fool most of the time when it came to Ivy because her mere existence took away all reason. Foolish or not, he didn't mind because she made it okay. He leaned his forehead to hers. "I'll do dinner. You work your magic with a few equations."

He caught her laugh in a kiss.

Thank you for reading Hold Me Close - I hope you loved Ivy & Owen's story!

Up next in the Lodge Series is Violet & Sawyer's story in Crazy For You. Sawyer Hamilton is a sexy, alpha SEAL who falls for Violet almost the moment he lays eyes on her. Of course, it's never that simple. "An absolutely stunning story!!!" Don't miss Sawyer's story!

For more swoony & sassy romance, check out my website for the following stories: https://jhcroixauthor.com/books/

This Crazy Love kicks off the Swoon Series - small town southern romance with enough heat to melt you! Jackson & Shay's story is epic - swoon-worthy & intensely emotional. Jackson just happens to be Shay's brother's best friend. He's also *seriously* easy on the eyes. Shay has a past, the kind of past she would most definitely like to forget. Past or not, Jackson is about to rock her world. Don't miss their story!
Free on all retailers!

Burn For Me is a second chance romance for the ages. Sexy firefighters? Check. Rugged men? Check. Wrapped up together? Check. Brave the fire in this hot, small-town romance. Amelia & Cade were high school sweethearts & then it all fell apart. When they cross paths again, it's epic - don't miss Cade's story!
Free on all retailers!

For more small town romance, take a visit to Last Frontier Lodge in Diamond Creek. A sexy, alpha SEAL meets his match with a brainy heroine in Take Me Home. Marley is all brains & Gage is all brawn. Sparks fly when their worlds collide. Don't miss Gage & Marley's story!
Free on all retailers!

If sports romance lights your spark, check out The Play. Liam is a British footballer who falls for Olivia, his doctor. A twist of forbidden heats up this swoon-worthy & laugh-out-loud romance. Don't miss Liam & Olivia's story.
Free on all retailers!

Sign up for my newsletter, so you can receive information about upcoming new releases & receive a FREE copy of one of my books: http://jhcroixauthor.com/subscribe/

FIND MY BOOKS

Thank you for reading Hold Me Close! I hope you enjoyed the story. If so, you can help other readers find my books in a variety of ways.

1) Write a review!
2) Sign up for my newsletter, so you can receive information about upcoming new releases & receive a FREE copy of one of my books: http://jhcroixauthor.com/subscribe/
3) Like and follow my Amazon Author page at https://amazon.com/author/jhcroix
4) Follow me on Bookbub at https://www.bookbub.com/authors/j-h-croix
5) Follow me on Instagram at https://www.instagram.com/jhcroix/
6) Like my Facebook page at https://www.facebook.com/jhcroix

* * *

Last Frontier Lodge Novels
Take Me Home
Love at Last
Just This Once
Falling Fast
Stay With Me
When We Fall
Hold Me Close
Crazy For You
Just Us
Dare With Me Series
Crash Into You
Evers & Afters
Come To Me
Back To Us
Swoon Series
This Crazy Love
Wait For Me
Break My Fall
Truly Madly Mine
Still Go Crazy
If We Dare
Steal My Heart
Into The Fire Series
Burn For Me
Slow Burn
Burn So Bad
Hot Mess
Burn So Good
Sweet Fire
Play With Fire
Melt With You
Burn For You
Crash & Burn
That Snowy Night

Brit Boys Sports Romance
The Play
Big Win
Out Of Bounds
Play Me
Naughty Wish
Diamond Creek Alaska Novels
When Love Comes
Follow Love
Love Unbroken
Love Untamed
Tumble Into Love
Christmas Nights

ACKNOWLEDGMENTS

To my amazing readers who humble me every day with their support and cheers! To my family for giving me the crazy courage it takes to write stories.

xoxo

J.H. Croix

ABOUT THE AUTHOR

USA Today Bestselling Author J. H. Croix lives in a small town in the historical farmlands of Maine with her husband and two spoiled dogs. Croix writes contemporary romance with sassy women and alpha men who aren't afraid to show some emotion. Her love for quirky small-towns and the characters that inhabit them shines through in her writing. Take a walk on the wild side of romance with her best-selling novels!

Places you can find me:
jhcroixauthor.com
jhcroix@jhcroix.com